According to Mary

Marianne Fredriksson

ORION

Typeset in Bembo by Deltatype Ltd, Birkenhead, Merseyside

Printed in Great Britain by
Clays Ltd, St Ives plc

The Orion Publishing Group Ltd
Orion House
5 Upper Saint Martin's Lane
London, WC2H 9EA

ıary

By the same author:

HANNA'S DAUGHTERS
SIMON & THE OAKS
INGE & MIRA

According to Mary

WHY MARY MAGDALENE?

Perhaps it began when I read Simone Weil's 'Letter to a Dominican'. As is known, she was a Catholic, but in her letters she is fiercely critical of Christianity. She primarily turns against the appalling claims of the church to possess the only real truth. In whose name through the ages has judged and condemned human beings.

How did Jesus, whose foremost message is forgiveness and mercy, become the judgmental god? How could his determined distancing himself from priests and those learned in the scriptures lay the foundations to a religion with such harsh regulations, domination, and hierarchy?

Simone Weil put into words the questions that have always upset me when I read the gospels with all their contradictions. She herself says that a correct understanding of our religion is impossible because the early days of Christian history are wrapped in mystery.

This interested me. I began to read theology, the history of religion, mythology, and Greek philosophy. Delighted and astonished, I devoted myself to Sophia, and daughter of God, Wisdom, whose preaching bears great similarities to that of Jesus.

I quite soon realised that many of the contradictions in Christianity go back to the conflict between the Judeo-Christian congregation in Jerusalem and the Apostles who wanted to take the new message to the 'heathens'. Jerusalem's Christians maintained that all those who wished to convert must first become Jews, obey all the hundreds of decrees in the laws, and be circumcised. The foreign missionaries, with Paul in the lead, were opposed to the Jewish congregation and, is known, won the battle. As always, the victors wrote the history, the evangelists. That was how we, for instance, were given the story that it was the Jews who killed the Son of God – with terrible consequences throughout history.

After a while, I started playing with an idea, or rather a daydream perhaps. Supposing there had been a free, clear-thinking person among his disciples, someone who was open, unprejudiced, and acquainted with both Jewish and Greek thinking. Briefly, someone who had 'ears to listen'.

One day I was looking for something in the Nag Hammadi Library and happened to come upon the fragment that remains of the gospel of Mary Magdalene. In it she accounts for what Jesus said in personal conversations with her – among them: 'Make no rules of life on this which I have revealed to you. Write no laws as the law-makers do.' And it struck me: here is perhaps someone with ears to listen, eyes to see, and a mind to understand. The disciple whom Jesus loved the most. And a woman with no power to influence.

That was how my Mary Magdalene was born.

Marianne Fredriksson

A correct understanding of Christianity
has become almost an impossibility for us
owing to the profound secrecy surrounding
the early history of the time.

Simone Weil in *The Person and the Sacred*

Part One

I

She heard him speaking in the marketplace in Antioch, the man called Simon, who came to be called Peter. He was the same as usual. The fisherman from the shore of Lake Gennesaret had kept his lofty figure and rock-like features. And his gaze, childish and shallow.

She also recognized some of his words.

Like an echo.

'Love one another,' said the man in the marketplace.

Jesus had said that. But only now had she realized that he had never understood how little love people have.

'Love one another.' The large man repeated the words, giving them a ring of law.

Then she could see that his gaze was ingenuous.

A moment later, Simon spoke of the light that was not to be hidden, and she thought with surprise that Jesus had not known that people were condemned to the shadows.

His own light dazzled him, she thought.

Perhaps that was why he chose the darkest of all deaths.

Then finally the prayer she knew so well. 'Our Father . . .' And the crowd dispersed. A mocking laugh or two could be heard, but they soon ceased. Simon Peter's words contained a luminosity, a reflection of what had once been said. But they had lost their mystery.

Was it a long time ago? Was it still going on? On her way home, she thought about how she had hated the big-mouthed fisherman, and was ashamed. So she tried to pray: 'Dear Lord, forgive me my wicked thoughts.'

Then she thought she should never have gone to the meeting. She should have known better. She had needed a great many years to forget, and she now no longer remembered Jesus' face, nor his hands, nor even his eyes or the mouth forming those amazing words. She had even banished the sweetness of the night from her memory. The smile was the most difficult. That could afflict her at any time in her everyday life.

A neighbouring wife had told her that a prophet from the new sect was to speak in the marketplace in the Jewish sector of the town.

'I'm curious, but daren't oppose my husband,' she had said.

'I'm curious about the new zealots, too,' Mary had replied, with a bitter smile as she remembered Simon Peter thrice denying the Lord.

As she was making breakfast, her curiosity overcame her and became compelling. I'll go. I'll put on my black mantle and a veil over my face. No one will recognize me.

It had gone well and no one had noticed her, a black crow among all the other black crows.

She could not sleep the night after the meeting, nor weep, although it was grief afflicting her, her heart, beating as if about to burst.

She got up and tried walking across the floor, but her legs would not carry her. For a while she tried blowing life into her old hatred of Simon and all those damned fishermen. And of Jesus himself, he who had preferred a cruel death to a life with her.

But her bitterness had gone.

Suddenly, with crystal clarity appeared the memory of her last meeting with the disciples in that dark hall in Jerusalem the man with the water jar had taken them to, the sun making its way through the high windows and weaving rays of glittering dust through the air. And the words, asking her, 'Give us the words he spoke to you and which we do not know.'

She could see now the men were weeping. How strange that she had forgotten their despair, she thought. Then she heard her own young voice.

'I saw the Lord in a vision and greeted him. He said: "Blessed are those who are not afraid of the sight of me. Wherever is your spirit lies the treasure." '

She was so eager, she failed to notice the faces of the men round the table clouding over, and untiringly she went on telling them what he had said.

' "Be of good cheer, the Son of Man is within you. Follow him, he who seeks him will find him. Write no laws of this that I have revealed to you. Write no laws as the scribes do." '

She was still talking, of death, of everything man had to overcome while his soul was still in his body: anger, desire, and ignorance. She repeated a conversation between body and soul: 'The body says, "I did not see you." And the soul replies, "I saw you. But you neither saw nor recognized me." I asked him, "What are the sins of the world?" And he answered me, "There is no sin in the world. You create it yourself when you falsify reality." '

That was when Peter had cried out, 'These are strange teachings.' Then he turned to the others. 'I don't believe our Lord spoke these words. Why should he speak privately with a woman and not openly with us?'

'Brother Peter. Do you think I would tell lies about the Lord?'

There, in bed in Antioch, she was at last able to weep. As the first dawn light was colouring the sky, she slept, an uneasy sleep disturbed by images from her wanderings round the blue lake, and it was long into the day when she woke and felt the weight of stones inside her.

But her heart was beating as it should and her head was quite clear.

That was when she knew she had to go the whole way back, break her way through overgrown paths, stung by nettles and slashed by the undergrowth.

She got up and as she washed, in her mind she could see his smile. He was encouraging her!

'But I'm only one human being,' she said aloud.

Then she sat down to pray and sent her prayer straight to the Son of Man.

'I have at last understood that you loved me with the love that embraces all. What confused me was the constant talk by the disciples about whom you loved best.

'You loved and perhaps felt gratitude for teaching you bodily love, so increasing your knowledge of the condition of humankind. Your mother tried to talk to you about the inescapable cruelty of life, but you did not listen. You did listen to me. With your body.

'God in heaven, how lonely you were.

'Yet I contributed to making you into a human being. But then you did not learn of the world of shadows until you were at the cross.

'I remember you were often surprised. "How can you see the splinter in your brother's eye and not see the beam in your own."

'I could have told you how great the fear was. But I was only twenty. And a whore.'

2

Mary had a great deal to do. Leonidas was to return home that day, thirsty, tired, and hungry. She put the great water pan to the fire and fetched water. As usual at the well, she glanced with gratitude up at the mountains in the south where Daphne's springs leapt out of the rocks and supplied the town with an abundance of clear fresh water.

They were expecting his sister in the afternoon. She was to bring the account book and the two of them were to sit at the big table to enter all the expenses and income from his journey.

'Please, God, that trade was good,' said Mary, but her words were largely routine, an unnecessary invocation out into the air. She liked her sister-in-law, but feared those bold eyes that saw straight through you.

Mary Magdalene had much to hide.

She should have gone to the market the day before. Now she had to hurry down to the marketplace. She was in luck – a large piece of fresh lamb, some smoked fish, and a basket of vegetables and fruit. On her way home she passed the synagogue, and for a moment wished she could go in to Rabbi Amasya and tell him her story, but the thought was only random.

She remembered her neighbour had said that Simon Peter and his companions were staying with the rabbi. She pulled down her headcloth and hurried on.

She managed to clean the house and fill her jars with flowers from the garden, then finally combed her long hair and fastened it into a long plait round her head. A golden crown; she was proud of her hair. But she was troubled when she looked in the mirror and saw how wide-open her eyes were, dark shadows all around them.

3

When Leonidas arrived, the house smelled of spices, flowers, and roasting lamb. He sniffed at the aroma and laughed aloud with delight. As usual, he took her two hands in his.

'Every evening on my journey,' he said, 'I try to remember how beautiful you are. But I have a poor imagination and you always surpass my images.'

'Silly. I'm beginning to grow old.'

'You'll never grow old.'

'The eyes of love,' she said, smiling, but then he noticed the dark circles around her eyes.

'Mary, something's happened.'

'This evening,' she said. 'We must have a long talk this evening. Now you must take a bath, then eat. Then Livia is coming.'

He groaned.

When he emerged from the bath, she saw what she did not want to see, that he had aged, that his supple body was gradually slackening and his dark hair had grey streaks in it.

They ate. The meat was tender and the wine red and heavy.

'You've time for a sleep before your sister comes.'

He nodded gratefully, disappeared into the bedroom and a moment later she heard him snoring.

When Livia arrived, Mary was washing the dishes.

'I can't think why you don't buy yourself a slave girl,' her sister-in-law said as usual.

Mary had the words on the tip of her tongue but kept her mouth shut. Livia would not have understood. 'Serve one another.'

'Some wine?' she said instead.

'Thank you, but I must keep my head clear. Give me some of that drink you brew from herbs instead.'

They went and sat in the garden with a goblet each, and looked at each other. She doesn't age, thought Livia. She is as young as the day she came. Just as fair. Dark blue eyes, still so clear, reflecting the good sense that the gods had given her. But she seldom uses it, simply goes around enclosed in her own strength.

She is not really beautiful, her nose too long and her mouth too small for that narrow face. And it reveals every shift in her vulnerability, in strange contrast to that forceful and penetrating gaze.

A flock of white storks with black wings flew over the garden on their way to the cold waters of the Teutons far away in the north. Livia watched them, thinking how free they were.

Then she looked searchingly at Mary.

'You look tired.'

'I slept badly last night.'

'Were you lonely?'

'Yes,' said Mary, relieved that she had not needed to lie.

She answers promptly to all questions, thought Livia, and manages to hide everything behind her simple words. She does not lie. She is too intelligent for that.

And yet she has great secrets.

A group of flamingos flapped over the rooftops, colouring the sky pink. This time it was Mary watching them.

'They came down along the river,' she said.

Livia was still thinking about her sister-in-law. Perhaps it is her secrets that give her strength; perhaps we would all have greater strength if we possessed a piece of inner land into which no one had access.

She sighed. She herself was like an open book.

She could see now that the darkness around Mary was denser than usual. Livia had long known her sister-in-law had bad memories. Leonidas had told her about her parents, the father crucified as a rebel and her mother and brothers hacked to death.

4

Jews. That stubborn people, thought Livia, insolent enough to maintain there was only one god and that he was theirs.

Fanatics.

But Mary did not seem particularly Jewish, noticeably fair-skinned and blonde as she was. And those eyes, a brilliant blue like the spring gentians flowering in the mountains. She did go to the synagogue, occasionally, but if she were religious, her faith was slight.

'There's a prophet in town, a Jew recruiting people to a new religion,' said Livia. 'Have you heard about him?'

Mary was saved from replying, for at that moment Leonidas appeared on the threshold. But both he and Lavia saw all colour in Mary's face drain away when she swayed slightly as she rose from the table.

'Please excuse me,' she said. 'I'm not feeling well.'

'Mary dear, go and rest.'

Leonidas followed her to the bed, looking worried. 'Who?' he whispered.

'Simon Peter.'

'We'll talk tonight.'

But there was no talking that night. Leonidas and Livia had decided to go to the marketplace to listen to the new prophet.

'I must be allowed to see him.'

'Mind neither he nor his companions recognize you.'

'You won't come with us?'

'No, I couldn't . . . not again.'

'You were there yesterday?'

'Yes.'

Livia had gone home to change. Like Mary, she chose black clothes and a large headcloth. When she returned to fetch them, she was told that Mary was still not feeling well.

'Anyhow, she's not interested in dreamy prophets,' said Leonidas. Livia realized her brother was less clever than his wife. He lied quite unnecessarily.

Leonidas came back late that night. Mary was asleep, but he found he could not sleep. All the incredible things he had heard were swirling around in his head, fantastic images interwoven into an incomprehensible legend. At dawn, he went into her room.

'We must have a talk now.'

She was less burdened than she had been the night before, but her heart was fluttering as if beating emptily in her chest.

She could see from his eyes that Leonidas was deeply disturbed and filled with rage. He said Simon Peter had turned into a great liar. The apostle had told a story that was all magical nonsense from various religions.

'What do you mean?'

'I'll tell you. Jesus was born of a virgin and conceived by God himself.'

He laughed.

'The god of the Jews has clearly begun to resemble the Zeus of the Greeks, seriously addicted to earthly virgins. Jesus came into the world in a stable in Bethlehem. It says in some old prophecy that the Messiah was to be born there. He is also descended in a direct line from King David, a family that died out a hundred years ago.'

He fell silent, thinking for a moment before going on.

'Some of these legends are taken from the Jewish scriptures, others just superstitious public property. It's all been woven together into a fantastic myth to confirm that Jesus was a god who out of compassion allowed himself to be born among people.'

Strangely enough, Mary was not surprised. He looked at her and said challengingly: 'Did you ever hear him saying he was the Messiah?'

'No, no. He called himself the Son of Man. I knew his mother, a good worldly woman. She was the widow of a carpenter in Nazareth, had many children and a hard life.'

Leonidas groaned before going on. 'After three days, Jesus rose from the dead. Like Osiris, Isis' husband. As you know, she also gave birth to a son of god.'

Mary was not interested in Osiris.

'Did the disciples see Jesus in a vision?'

'No, his body. They could feel the scars from the wounds he got on the cross. After forty days, he went to heaven and he'll soon be returning to judge us all.'

'Jesus never judged,' whispered Mary. 'He judged no one, neither publicans, whores, nor other wretches.'

Leonidas was not listening, and went on. 'According to Peter, he died for our sins. We were to be cleansed by his blood. He sacrificed himself like a sacrificial lamb, the kind the Jews slaughter in their bloodstained temple.'

She tried to calm her heart. Then she remembered.

'He said we had to take up our cross and follow him.'

They sat in silence for quite a while before Mary resumed.

'It's true he chose his death, but people didn't understand him. Neither then, nor now.'

She looked at Leonidas, so certain in his interpretations. She herself held no opinions, but thought that if you sought to understand Jesus, it was not at all strange that you took strength from all the dreams the world had dreamt from the very beginning of time.

Then she remembered the old prayers she had heard as a child in the synagogue in Magdala, about he who was to come to awaken the dead, succour the fallen, cure the sick, free the captives, and be faithful to those sleeping in the dust.

'They call themselves Christian and have adherents everywhere,' said Leonidas. 'With the help of these legends, they could be successful.'

Again they sat in silence.

Mary finally found the courage to speak of all the thoughts she had had during that difficult night – that she should go back into her memory and give expression to every word and every action from the years of wandering with the Son of Man.

Leonidas grew eager. 'Write, write down everything you can remember. After all, you were the one closest to him, and knew him best.'

Mary shook her head, thinking no one had known him, and every one of His followers had understood him in his own way.

'It'll be difficult,' she said. 'He was too great for us.'

Toward evening, as agreed, they went to Livia's to a welcome home dinner she had invited them to. They took the route around the handsome Daphne portal, and while Leonidas went to check that his goods had gone through customs, Mary climbed the steep steps in the town wall to look out over the huge caravan camp. Thousands of sheds and tents extended across the plain until they vanished over the horizon. Hundreds of camels were swaying along the alleys between tents, sheds, and the throngs of people in exotic clothing. The distance was too great for her to be able to hear what they were shouting, but that did not matter, for she knew she would not understand those foreign tongues.

Mary let her gaze roam to the west, following the long stony fortress out toward the sea and the harbour town of Seleucia. She saw the poor quarters clinging to the wall and thought about the exhausted drunken men, the whores trying to survive by selling their bodies, the children begging and rummaging in the garbage from the ships.

It was an unbearable world and she firmly turned her eyes in the other direction. There she could just make out the caravan route across the mountains. Slowly, day after day, it would wind its way eastward toward the Euphrates and on toward the heart of the kingdom of Parthia.

When Leonidas came to fetch her, he was pleased, for all had gone as expected, but he was muttering as usual about the high cost of the tolls.

Livia lived by the shore of the Orontes, not far from the river island where the Seleucians had built their palace. As they sat down at table, they could hear the murmur of the sluggishly flowing river and watch the evening birds settling along the shores for the night. Livia's daughter and her husband were also there. Mary greeted Mera with great warmth, a young woman with a confident relationship to God. She worshipped Isis and was daily absorbed in prayer before the great goddess' stone in the temple.

As always at Livia's, the food was exquisite, but that had no effect on Leonidas, who was short-tempered and gritty-eyed.

But his sister was filled with the previous evening, impressed by Simon Peter, and she spoke eloquently of the tremendous force radiating from the man.

'He must have been amazing, that young prophet in Palestine,' she said. 'I thought there was something moving about the stories about his virtues, something gentle and innocent.'

Mary was surprised. So that was what Livia had heard. For a moment she was tempted to confide in her, but a look from Leonidas stopped her. Then, Livia went on.

'As far as I can make out, his teaching is much like that of Orpheus. And these new Christians do resemble many other fraternities of slaves and the poor all over the Roman Empire, where everyone is indifferent to their sufferings.'

'You forget that those slaves and the poor are in a dangerous majority,' said Nicomachus, her son-in-law.

'But he was no revolutionary, this young prophet.'

'He was crucified as a troublemaker, anyhow.'

Livia was not listening.

'It seemed to me,' she went on, 'that he . . . whatever his

name was ... yes, Jesus, refused to see that people are fundamentally evil. He was naive.'

Mary wanted to cry out that Jesus was much greater than Livia would ever understand, but she made herself keep quiet, remembering that she herself had had similar thoughts. 'His light was so strong, he found it difficult to see clearly.'

Simon Peter stayed for a few more days, speaking in the handsome public square at Antioch. He was successful, and the first large Christian congregation outside Jerusalem was founded.

But Mary did not go to his meetings.

5

Mary found remembering difficult. Day after day, she found herself sitting in front of her empty papyrus roll.

'Don't bother about the sequence of events,' Leonidas said. 'Just start with an event whenever it happened.'

Again she tried to capture the scene in the house in Jerusalem at the time when Simon Peter had repudiated her. Then she remembered what Andrew, Simon's brother, had said the moment she had stopped speaking.

'What strange things you are preaching. And I don't believe you.'

The next moment, Simon spoke the contemptuous words that Jesus did not speak privately with a woman. But then she remembered there had been another voice.

'You're hot tempered, Simon. Now you're fighting with the woman as if with an enemy. If the Saviour found her worthy, who are you to judge her? He sensed her spirit, so was able to give her knowledge that we wouldn't have understood.'

Jesus had said that. The gentle Levi had said those words. Why had she forgotten them?

Mary's heart filled with pride, and she went out into the garden to delight in every flower.

What was it Jesus had seen in her?

She knew that the tremendous question of just who he was would never be answered. All she could do was to give her testimony on what was incomprehensible insofar as she had understood it. But to do that, she first had to know who she herself was. She would take Leonidas' advice and start from the beginning.

She was born in Magdala on the shores of the Gennesaret, her village poor, the people scraping a living from the meagre fields, and the lake, which was rich in fish. Sheep and goats grazed on the dry hillsides. Mary was not yet five when she was sent to watch the animals on the slopes round the village. Her mother warned her not to go in among the trees higher up the slopes. There beneath the terebinth trees and among the grey trunks of old oaks, wild dogs and the laughing hyena lay in wait, greedy for human flesh.

Mary was an obedient child, but was occasionally defiant and went into the forest, where it was quiet and dignified in the shimmering foliage beneath the trees. The child realized that that was where God lived.

God was often talked about at home. Every winter morning she heard her father thanking the Almighty: 'Praise be to Thee, oh Lord, King of the Universe, for not creating me a woman.' And her mother's voice answering: 'Praise be to Thee, Lord, for creating me according to Thy will.'

The father never looked at the girl, but past her or through her, as if she did not exist. She was afraid of him, the darkness that surrounded his coarse figure, and that closed face with its hard eyes.

It was a relief when spring came, not just because of the warmth and the flowers, but because it never failed that as the breeze rocked the red anemones on the hillsides, and whenever her father went away, a great peace fell over their home. 'Where does he go?'

Her mother's reply was always the same. 'Up into the mountains.' She said it with pursed lips, as if reluctant to let the words out, and the girl realized she should ask no more questions.

But her mother was also more lighthearted after her husband had gone. Not that she showed it, and perhaps Mary was the only one to know her secret. When the two of them went to the well to fetch water, they might stop on the way and look up at the mountains where the oleanders were flowering pink among the honeysuckle and broom. If the child asked properly, she could persuade her mother to read aloud from the scriptures.

'For lo, the winter is past, the rain is over and gone. The flowers appear on the earth; the time of the singing of birds is come and the voice of the turtle is heard in our land. The fig tree putteth forth her green figs, and the vines with their tender grape give a good smell . . .'

Then they smiled at each other.

Mary's family owned neither fishing boat nor vineyards, but they had one great wealth – the largest fig tree in the village growing outside the door of their house. This blessed tree with its thousand green fingers gave shade during the hot summer and was generous to the poor, providing two crops each year. In mild springs, the first sweet figs might ripen as early as at Passover, then toward winter, before the rainstorms came, the fruit on that year's shoots ripened and were carefully, almost reverently, gathered from the tree.

Her mother gave birth to a child every summer, four sons in an equal number of years, the births always occurring most inappropriately in the middle of harvest. She gave birth without a whimper and was back in the fields again a few days later, a new child in a bag on her back. The neighbours helped as best they could, but not until after the new son had been circumcised.

It was when the latest infant was ill with a high fever after circumcision and was being cared for by Mary that she noticed for the first time that her father was not the only one who looked away from her – no, the neighbours, too, even her mother's brother behaved as if she did not exist. She understood then that it was a curse to be born a girl, and in addition the firstborn.

But that was also not the whole explanation for her becoming an outsider.

Then there was the headcloth. The other little girls were allowed to let the cloth down when the wind cooled the work in the fields. But not Mary. Every morning, as soon as her mother had rolled up the sleeping mats, she brushed Mary's hair, wound it into a hard plait and pulled the cloth tightly around her little head, then finally tied the knot under her chin, so hard the child could not possibly untie it.

The girl was ashamed of her hair. Once when she was alone among the sheep, she managed to ease the cloth down over her shoulders and pull a strand of her hair out of the plait. She was frightened and saw with horror that her hair was unnatural, as yellow as ripe wheat. From that day on she no longer complained about her headcloth – on the contrary, she helped tie the knot even harder and pushed the cloth down over her forehead so far that the hairline was hidden.

Her mother sighed in the mornings as she plaited Mary's hair. One day she said that the headcloth served no purpose as long as it could not hide the girl's eyes.

'What's wrong with my eyes?'

'They're beautiful,' her mother said, flushing. 'Blue as the spring irises in the field.'

For a moment Mary sensed a suppressed longing in her mother's voice. It was strange, but she realized that in some secretive way it was to do with her and the bond between the two of them. No one else could see it, but Mary knew that she was the child her mother loved most. She was the one who had a piece of newly baked bread secretly slipped to her, and sometimes when they were alone in the stable, her mother gave her the rich top layer of the milk.

She felt comforted now – she had beautiful eyes. But that very same afternoon, she began secretly looking into the eyes of the other children. Some were so dark the pupil was impossible to distinguish, but most were various shades of brown. One or two were lighter, one boy's actually grey, and when she looked more carefully, she found his hair was also lighter than the others. Not as horribly yellow as hers, but when the sun shone on it, it could glint like silver.

Only once did she see a man with blue eyes. That was when a troop of Romans rode through the village and people cowered inside their houses, pale with bitterness and fear. The soldiers rode close to the houses, and, peering round from the stable, Mary suddenly met the eyes of a young soldier, eyes as blue as the sky, and beneath his helmet a glimpse of his hair – yellow like hers.

A moment later, he had passed, but it made a deep impression on her. She looked like the hated strangers!

Some time later, she happened to overhear a conversation between a neighbour, Abiathar, and one of his sons. They were talking about the Romans who had come riding through the village and the Jewish rebels gathering in increasing numbers in the mountains to practise the art of war. The young man wanted to join them.

'God wishes his people to be free.'

'Only madmen follow Judas of Galilee into the mountains. Crazy men like Barak. He's left his wife and children to look after themselves and thinks we can throw the Romans out.'

'But God wishes . . .'

'God wishes that his people shall suffer and wait. When he finds the time is ripe, he will give us a sign. And he has not done that, either now or before the other wars. No miracles occur here.'

He raised his voice to a shout.

'Rebellion leads to slaughter, women and children murdered, fields and villages burned. And those heroes in the mountains are crucified.'

He spat out the last word as they walked on and Mary dared emerge from the undergrowth where she had been listening. She ran as fast as she could to her mother, who was just lighting the oil lamp.

'Mother, is there going to be war?'

'Where did you hear that?'

'Is father a warrior practising in the mountains?'

Her mother had never lifted her hand to Mary before, but now she struck her hard across the face. 'That's dangerous talk, Mary. Never, never must you pass it on, not to a single person.'

Mary rubbed her cheek, the tears flowing. Her mother pulled herself together. 'Let us pray for peace. But first you must promise me by God's holy scripts never again to take such talk on your tongue.'

The child wept and promised. But during prayers, she sat silently, and behind her tightly closed eyes she reckoned what Abiathar had said to his son must be true. 'Women and children murdered, fields and villages burned. And the heroes in the mountains crucified.'

Why otherwise would her mother be in such despair?

The next day, Abiathar's son had gone and the child could see the fear in people's faces. But they said nothing, as if it were risky even to speak of the danger. Silence settled on the village and behind it, rancour and suspicion grew. People greeted each other, but no longer stopped to exchange words.

Mary's mother had always been lonely, and now they excluded Barak's wife from the community.

One day the girl met an old herdsman, a taciturn man she knew, who seldom opened his mouth. He drove his sheep past hers and glanced at her.

'Oh yes,' he said. 'It's happened before and will happen again.'

News trickled into the village, some from the shepherds who met other herdsmen in the mountains. But most came by boat, strangers who had fled on board the fishing boats across the lake. Some spoke of victories, successful ambushes. But their words were vague and their eyes without hope. Others told of great battles and thousands of crucified Jews.

The old herdsman came down from the mountains and told them that Varius, the Roman general and governor of Syria, was on his way with two legions. The one army was going around the lake and attacking from the south, while the other had chosen the route across the mountains in the north.

'We'll be crushed between two walls,' he said.

Mary listened without understanding.

A few days later, when she had been sent to the shore to buy fish, an old fisherman shouted at her to go away, for she was defiling the catch. She went home with the coin clasped in her hand and her body rigid with terror.

'I defiled their fish.'

Her mother seemed to turn to stone, but her eldest brother, then five, cried out that Mary had brought shame on the family.

'Everyone says you're unclean, a child of sin,' he shouted. But that broke their mother's paralysis.

'If Mary is a child of sin, then I am a whore,' she said, her voice hard and her eyes burning with fury as she shook the boy. 'Have you forgotten how God judges he who does not honour his parents?'

Mary did not know what a whore was, but at that moment

understood that the evil afflicting her family was all her fault. That was when she decided to run away.

During the following nights, she gathered up all her strength. She would wait for a moonless night and walk to the new town Herod Agrippa had had built in honour of the Roman emperor. Herod called it Tiberias and the Jews called it the City of Sin.

Mary wept sometimes, but only a little and only when she thought about her mother.

Then at last it was a night with no moon. It was difficult walking in the dark and she fell several times, grazing her knees, then wiping the blood away with the mantle she had thrown over her shoulders. With horror she realized that although she had gone only a short way along the road, she would have to stop and rest until dawn. She shook off the cold, but that was not what kept her awake. No, there were strange noises filling the night.

Angels of Satan, she thought. Then it is true that Lucifer's followers roar in the mountains on nights when the moon is resting.

She could hear the sound of horses' hooves in the mountains, hundreds of horses, a little later the rattle of swords coming toward her, yells from men as blows struck helmets, shouted orders and victorious cries.

It dawned on her then that war was upon them.

She had to get back to Mother.

Mary ran as she had never run before, the sky red in the north, so that could not be the dawn.

Seopharis was burning.

She could just glimpse the first houses in Magdala, still dark and calm, but she stopped outside the door when to her surprise, she heard her father's voice, angry and raucous.

'You say nothing, woman.'

'Go back into the mountains. They're after you and you lead them straight to me and the children. Go! Go on!'

'Have you forgotten what the scriptures say about the woman who rebels against her husband?'

He was bellowing like a madman, so loudly that he did not hear the clatter of the Roman troops' horses. But Mary heard it and without even thinking, she slipped away. The house had only three stone walls, the fourth the rock it leaned against, with a narrow opening in the far corner between rock and wall and a ladder up to the roof. She climbed halfway up, knowing dawn would soon be coming and she would be visible on the roof.

She stayed there between the hillside and the ladder, and through a crack, she was able to see down into the room when the soldiers broke down the door. Laughing, they struck her father in the face and trussed him up, winding the rope around him from his feet up over his belly, chest, and arms, until he looked like a large fish, the kind you tie up before smoking them.

'To the cross with you.'

That was a Greek speaking broken Aramaic.

Then the soldiers caught sight of the woman and the small children.

'Leave them be.'

'No, we're to exterminate the Jews as we do vermin.'

Mary closed her eyes tight as they slit the throats of her mother and brothers, only one thought now left in her head. She wanted to die.

But she didn't know how to. She kept her eyes closed, then smelt smoke.

They had set fire to the house.

Without thinking and without really wanting to, Mary fled, up toward the mountain, where she came to the old goat path, then she ran and ran and ran.

6

At home in Antioch, Mary Magdalene was making a supreme effort to recall those difficult images. What is true? What is fiction? Where does the boundary run? How much can anyone remember without falling apart?

She had no more memories. She had simply shut her eyes and run.

She had also continued to keep her eyes shut over all those years with Euphrosyne. But she had been frightened of the nights, when what had been forgotten appeared to her in the dark.

Though on the whole, she had largely succeeded in her aim: never to remember. Until she had met Jesus, and he had said: 'Only the truth can free you.'

The truth? She looked at the scroll where she had written down the story of her childhood. Then the question returned: How much of it was true?

Had she gilded her childhood? No, even the most difficult upbringing has its brighter memories. A child requires so little, sun playing in the leaves of the trees, a newborn lamb sleeping in her arms, but also the joy of movement, leaping over stones and running over mountains.

Had she exaggerated her alienation?

She did not think so. She could still feel the shame of her yellow hair and her blue eyes. And the contempt she had faced.

Once again she read through what she had written, thinking in the way she thought about Jesus: how alone she was. But she could now also see that she had been a strong and robust child, that girl in Magdala.

Mother.

She had taken pains, racking her memory to remember her mother's name. In vain. She could remember her mother's smile, probably because it was so rare. But the clearest pictures were of her mother's sorrow. And her exhaustion, her body sucked dry from childbearing, bowed, its beauty gone, and the clenched hand pressed to her back to ease the pain.

It was slavery, she thought.

Naturally she had not seen this as a child. In that world, the scriptures, the years of children were a woman's lot, what life was about and the will of God. Many of the children died, disappearing like shadows and forgotten. Just like the mothers deprived of their lives by childbirth.

Mother was sixteen years old when she gave birth to me, twenty-two when she died.

Mary was tired when she went to bed. As she closed the shutter, she saw the night was dark over the mountains, yet another moonless night.

That night, she prayed for dreamless sleep, but her prayers went unheard. She dreamt about Chua. Even in her sleep she felt surprise, a woman, the wife of her uncle, Mother's brother, coming toward her on the sheep track over the mountain, her arms held open to the girl, then hugging her, making her laugh.

When Mary woke, she felt light from the warmth of the dream. That must have happened, and the dream now clarified. Chua had been tall and proud, her breasts round, not flat as rolled-out dough. But then she had given birth to only three children, two sons and a daughter.

Then she had been let off.

Rumours about her had been mumbled by the women around the well and at the quay where they fetched the fish. Woman-talk, as envious as judgmental: she made horrible brews of herbs and drank them, an art she had learned from Lucifer. One woman had actually seen one of his evil angels visiting her.

They said she was arrogant, but she had been the only one to be kind to Mother and me. Mary could suddenly remember the quiet talk by the oven as the two women did their baking.

25

The next morning, as she sat down and took out her writing materials, she realized that in the future she would have to rely largely on Leonidas' memories.

7

He had been wounded in battle, Leonidas, the Greek and centurion. Not seriously, but he had bled profusely and he was grateful and greatly relieved to be ordered to return to the doctor in Tiberias.

He detested his actions, but even more the overflowingly emotional Jews, with their hair splitting, their terrible rhetoric, and their fearful tribal god.

He was riding at dawn as quietly as he could through inhospitable landscape, the screams of the crucified still ringing in his ears, when he suddenly caught sight of a child running along the path, swift little feet and long, unusually fair hair flying like wings from the little head.

'Hello there, who are you?'

The girl stopped and stared wide-eyed at the rider. Blue eyes!

'I am Mary from Magdala.'

Then she collapsed. He dismounted and picked the child up. There was no doubt she had lost consciousness. What in all the gods was he to do with her? She had spoken Aramaic, so she must be Jewish after all.

As he lifted her up on to the horse, he puzzled over his own actions. One Jewish child more or less, why should he bother?

Then he knew it was something to do with her eyes.

An hour later, he was knocking on the door of Euphrosyne's house of pleasure, beautifully situated on the lakeshore in the new town. She opened the door herself.

'Leonidas!' she exclaimed. 'You know perfectly well we're closed in the mornings. And I haven't had time to find a new boy for you.'

'Now listen. I've found a child and I want you to look after her on my behalf.'

Euphrosyne looked suspiciously at him.

'Her?' she said. 'Is it a girl?'

'Yes, and an unusual girl. I'll pay for her.'

'Have you deserted?'

'No, no. I was wounded in battle and sent back.'

He put the unconscious child into Euphrosyne's arms. Euphrosyne unwound the mantle she was wrapped in.

'An unusual child indeed,' she said in astonishment.

Mary emerged from her daze when she heard that light female voice, and stared at the handsome woman, thinking she must be either an angel of God or one of Lucifer's. Euphrosyne met the child's eyes and in her turn thought she had never seen such eyes before.

'I rely on you,' said Leonidas. 'And I'll pay you well.'

'Go and get your wounds seen to.'

At this stage, the whole house had woken and young women were standing in amazement around the child, all talking at once: 'How pretty she is, how enchanting. And how dirty!'

Mary was lowered into a bath of warm water smelling of spring flowers. She was not afraid of water, but was ashamed of her nakedness. And yet she knew she was in heaven and that was what they did there with the unclean.

Then she was dried with soft towels and put on a bed. That frightened her more than the bath, for she had never slept in a bed before. She was given a piece of bread with herb-spiced yogurt on it. And hot milk with honey, she could taste that, but also something else, a bitter flavour that was still on her tongue as she fell asleep.

She slept all that long day, but was awakened toward night by music and laughter. Euphrosyne had put the child's bed in her own room and left young Miriam to keep watch over her.

'She must have someone to turn to when she wakes. And you're the only one who can speak Aramaic.'

Miriam was grateful. She dozed off now and again, then fell asleep and woke from the sense that someone was watching her. Mary had been gazing at her for some time, at the fine Jewish face, the nobly curved nose, red lips, and long brown curly hair. Just the kind Mary had always wanted to have.

As Miriam shook herself awake, Mary pretended to be asleep, needing time to try to remember where she was, and she had to think about why this beautiful girl looked so sad. Then she began to weep in despair. She wanted to scream but nothing came but a whisper: 'Mother, they killed Mother.'

'There, there,' said Miriam, drying her tears and quietly calming her. 'Your mother is with God. All is well with her now.'

'Where am I?'

Miriam hesitated, but in the end told the truth. 'In Euphrosyne's house of pleasure.'

'Is that why they're playing so beautifully?'

'Yes, you could say that.'

'But you're not happy. You're sad.'

'I miss my mother, just as you do.'

Then Miriam did something she would probably be scolded for. She crept into bed with the child and drew her to her. As the dawn light shimmered over the lake, Euphrosyne found them both sleeping soundly, and gratefully, she took the opportunity to rest herself. It had been a troublesome night.

The house slept until the sun reached midday height, the silence occasionally broken by a woman's shrill voice whimpering, or praying to one of the many gods of eastern countries. Mary was sometimes awakened by the voices, but soon fell asleep again, not wanting to, not wanting . . .

Then everyone seemed to wake at once, laughter and cries filling the rooms, water splashing and more and more calls for something to eat.

By all the gods, they were hungry. The slaves had cleaned the house and there was no sign of the activities of the night.

Mary would never forget some of the events of that first day.

The person cooking the food was a man!

And you could eat as much as you liked.

They pressed it on her.

'Have some more bread. Have you tasted the chicken? Here's a bit of breast. Try the cheese, no, perhaps that's too strong for you. But here's something you'll like, fig cake with honey and dried grapes.'

She was praised for every mouthful she took . . . clever girl.

There were other peculiar things, too. Mary nearly choked when she noticed the woman beside her had yellow hair. And blue eyes!

Then she noticed that Euphrosyne herself was blue-eyed, but the most astonishing thing of all was her hair, gleaming red like fire.

They were all interested in the child, and when they realized she could not understand their language, they turned to Euphrosyne.

'She can stay, can't she? We'll make new clothes for her. She's so enchanting, we can teach her . . .'

Euphrosyne answered evasively. 'She's Leonidas' child,' she said.

The women laughed. Leonidas, the lover of boys, couldn't have made a woman with child!

'No, I think he found her in the mountains, escaping from the war.'

After their meal, they all disappeared out into the garden, Mary holding Miriam's hand. Euphrosyne shut herself into her room to count the money and enter the night's takings into the accounts. As so often, she had worries of her own – one of the girls had been mistreated, and seeing her injuries, Euphrosyne, had sent the slave boy to fetch the doctor.

When the doctor came, he might just as well examine the girl too, she thought, at heart wanting to be rid of her, for this was no place for a child, but at the same time, like the others in the house, she was greatly taken with her. There was something inexpressibly attractive about her, bright and secretive at the same time.

Well, it's Leonidas' problem, she said to herself. If he wants her to stay here, he'll have to be prepared to pay quite a bit. Miriam would have to be assigned to look after her, teach her to speak properly and behave decently. A few table manners, among other things; my goodness, the way she ate!

Euphrosyne spent some time reckoning out how much the loss of Miriam's services would cost her.

The big garden on the slope down to the lake took Mary's breath away. Never could she have dreamed of anything like it: birds singing in green thickets, flowers of the most amazing kinds glowing, hedges as high as walls making spaces to hide in, and springs rippling glittering water over elaborate mosaics. Down by the lake was a tree she recognized, a large terebinth, heavy with age and its secrets.

She reckoned it greeted her.

Most beautiful of all were the roses, their heavy silken heads white, yellow, and shimmering pink, though most were a deep, mysterious crimson.

She found the courage to ask.

'What are those flowers called?'

Miriam hesitated, for she knew no Aramaic word for roses, so it came about that rose was the first Greek word Mary learned.

On the way up from the garden, they met Euphrosyne, who told Miriam she must speak Greek. For the time being, Mary could ask questions in Aramaic, but Miriam was to give all the answers in Greek. Miriam's first thought was to protest that that was impossible, but no one opposed Euphrosyne.

'Go in now and show Mary around the house.'

The two girls pattered cautiously into the big hall, where the feasts were held, as Miriam put it. Mary thought it all indescribably grand, flowery rugs on the floor, wide divans, and stools with gilded legs. The walls were covered with mirrors, which frightened and fascinated her. She had once borrowed her mother's sliver of mirror, but had also learned that it was an abomination to look upon your own image. She had done so only that once, the day her mother had said that Mary's eyes were as blue as the irises.

Here she could not turn in any direction without seeing her own reflection, her whole body, perfectly clearly. And her face, her long nose, silly mouth, and horrid white skin. She gazed into her own eyes and found they were no bluer than Euphrosyne's.

'Can't you see now how pretty you are?' whispered Miriam in Aramaic.

But Mary could not; no, she shook her head, then gazed at Miriam's face in the mirror and at Miriam herself, amazed to find the two were exactly the same.

Toward afternoon, an old man came and squeezed her all over and looked long into the whites of her eyes. He did not frighten her, for he spoke kindly in her own language, then announced she was perfectly healthy.

A moment later Leonidas appeared, his arm now bandaged. He looked with delight at this fair child, now in a new pale blue tunic. He was suddenly inordinately pleased with his decision.

Mary dimly recognized the man on the horse, but dared not open her mouth, afraid of releasing the tears welling up in her throat.

'We'll be friends, you and I,' he said in his peculiar Aramaic. 'I'll be your new father.'

Then Mary could no longer stop the tears filling her eyes.

Euphrosyne told him he was going too fast. That made Leonidas feel like a clumsy ox, but then Miriam intervened and told them how Mary talked in her sleep and how the most horrible nightmares kept waking her up. From all this incoherent talk, Miriam had gathered that her mother and all her siblings had been slaughtered.

'Ask about her father.'

Miriam hesitated but then asked the question, and they saw the small face hardening.

'They took him and crucified him,' she said.

Not in so many words, but her expression told them she considered his death justified.

'She must have been afraid of him,' said Miriam.

'You'll have to wait a while before you take on the role of father,' said Euphrosyne.

Later on, Euphrosyne and Leonidas settled matters between them in the office, Leonidas agreeing to her conditions. He would pay for the child as well as the time Miriam would have to spend with Mary. As soon as she could speak passable Greek, he would find a teacher for her, for she was to have a Greek education. And he said she was to learn to read and write in Latin.

Then he stopped for a moment, before going on.

'She's not to be a whore.'

'Then you must take her away from here before she bleeds for the first time.'

As Leonidas rode away, he made his plans. He would be released from service with the Romans in a few years, and then he would return home with a little daughter.

How astonished they would be, his family in Antioch.

8

One day Mary was reading through what she had written as usual, when she suddenly felt an unexpected tenderness toward this child, snatched away from a primitive peasant village and thrown into an enchanted world.

How much time had gone by before the girl understood?

Not long, she reckoned. First of all, there was Miriam and her misery, dark as an abyss. Then of course there was the language. The child had learned quickly, as children do, and she listened with increasing astonishment, not only to the strange cries slicing through her sleep at night, but also at their midday meal around the great table in the kitchen, when the women exchanged views on the night's guests and their experiences – complaining, laughing, and weeping.

They despised and mocked the men who rang the doorbell of the house at regular intervals. Why? Mary could not make it out, and found it difficult to put together all the stories she heard.

She remembered trying to ask Miriam. Miriam replied by weeping, twisting her hands and rushing out of their bedroom. That was when Mary decided to get up in the middle of the night and slip down to the big room on the ground floor to see for herself. But Euphrosyne caught her, clipped her over the ear, and roughly carried her back to her own room.

The next day Euphrosyne had a long talk with her.

In her room in Antioch, Mary sat thinking: Tomorrow I shall try to remember what she said.

They each sat on a velvet-covered stool in Euphrosyne's office, Euphrosyne sometimes taking Mary's hand in hers, but otherwise, as always, quite unemotional.

She began by telling Mary how children came about, how the man put his member into the woman's vagina and filled it with semen. That was nothing unusual to Mary. She had seen goats and sheep copulating and she could vaguely remember nights when she was awakened by her father's groans as he penetrated his wife.

Euphrosyne called it intercourse, then said it was a great pleasure. That surprised Mary.

'For many it's the only way of being close to another person,' Euphrosyne went on, smiling, which she often did, her smile somehow never quite complete. 'That's why they call it love,' she went on with a laugh.

The girl looked at her with surprise, for she had never seen anyone laughing with the corners of her mouth turned down like that.

Euphrosyne paused, as if needing time to choose her lies, for there were limits to what could be said to a seven-year-old about follies and perversions.

'There are women who find great joy in sleeping with a man,' she said. 'The girls who work here with me are often that kind.'

Mary thought about her mother. Had she liked it? And she noticed there was some hesitation in Euphrosyne's voice.

'Miriam,' she whispered.

Euphrosyne sighed and admitted it straight out.

'The Jewish girls often have problems.'

She paused again, thinking about the Jewesses she had had, girls full of anguish and feelings of guilt. When they painted themselves for the evening, she had heard them gabbling desperate prayers to the god who alone rules over the hearts of the Jews. But how much could she say to this Jewish child? She hesitated again before going on.

'They've been brought up to believe it is mortal sin to sleep with a man they are not married to. They call us whores. We are unclean in their eyes.'

Mary made an effort to understand, but her memories kept intruding – Mother's voice – 'If Mary is a child of sin, then I'm a whore.' In a firm voice, and looking Euphrosyne straight in the eyes, Mary said, 'I am unclean.'

Euphrosyne tried to hide her surprise. 'You're an innocent child. I can't think why you imagine you're unclean.'

'They told me I was.'

In the long silence that followed, the first autumn rains began to fall on the roses in the garden. The girl noticed. 'Why do people grow roses?' she said in a worried voice.

'Because they're beautiful, my child. The rose is also the flower of love, so it is appropriate here. What we do here could be called acts of love.'

Yet another crooked smile, but at that moment, the child believed her. Euphrosyne had that rare ability to be herself, and that invoked trust. She was often exposed to the anger of the women. After difficult nights, they could scream at her that she was heartless, that she exploited them, and they hated her.

But they trusted her.

After a long silence, Mary said, 'But why don't you let Miriam go if she's unhappy?'

'She has nowhere to go. She was raped by a soldier and gave birth to a child in secret. Her parents put the child out and drove Miriam away.'

Euphrosyne had been speaking in broken Aramaic and Mary was not sure she had understood correctly. She made an effort to remember word for word what they had said as she walked slowly to the secret cave on the shore where Miriam was waiting. It had stopped raining and a rainbow was arching high over the blue lake.

Miriam flushed with indignation when Mary told her about the acts of love in the house of pleasure.

'She's lying,' said Miriam. 'This is a house of sin, where they sell women's bodies at a high price. Whores, that's what we are. So watch out, Mary, so you don't go the same way as I have.'

Mary sat in silence, looking along the shore at the vapour rising from the warm baths where the soldiers were.

'You must know they are lackeys of Satan,' said Miriam, following Mary's gaze over toward the bathhouse.

All this was very confusing to Mary. Her thoughts went back to how she had learned to hate Romans and Greeks, and to the blue-eyed soldier riding past her home, and to Leonidas, who was so kind. As if reading her thoughts, Miriam said, 'They are godless, like all foreigners.'

'Serena prays to God. I've heard her myself.'

'Serena is a Philistine.' Miriam spat out the word. 'Her god is an idol, a goddess,' she whispered into Mary's ear.

That frightened Mary. A goddess, that was truly terrible.

She dared not tell Miriam what Euphrosyne had said about her. Maybe that was also a lie. But she reckoned it was probably true, for there must be some explanation for the lovely girl's grief.

Relations between the two of them became more and more complex, Miriam at times hating Mary because she learned Greek so quickly. The child would soon no longer need her, and that meant she would have to go back 'to work,' as Euphrosyne put it.

Mary sensed the other girl's anger, but was unable to understand it. She was proud of her progress and all the praise she received because she was so clever.

'She's gifted, has a good head, is ambitious,' the women kept saying at the dinner table.

She learned to read and write, but Miriam's spelling was weak, so Leonidas was displeased.

Some time went by.

Euphrosyne excused Miriam from her teaching duties after the arrival of the new teacher who came to teach Mary Greek and Latin. Erigones disliked his assignment, but as a slave, he had no choice when his owner, a Roman tribune, loaned him to Leonidas.

For Mary, this was the end of playing at learning. She now sat every morning in Euphrosyne's office together with a man with a harsh expression and fierce demands. Latin was beautiful, although at first the grammar tied her brain into knots.

What she liked best was when he read the Greek tales to her, choosing one a day, then telling her to write it down freely during the afternoon. She wrote about Perseus slaying the Gorgon after tremendous adventures; and Aesculapius, son of Apollo and beautiful Coronis, the father of medicine; and about the terrible voyage of the Argonauts when Jason stole the Golden Fleece.

But the story she liked best was about Persephone and Demeter, the girl abducted by the harsh ruler of the underworld. Mary wept with pity for the mother roaming the world in search of her daughter.

Miriam and Mary still shared a room, but their confidential talks became fewer, and Miriam shuddered with horror when Mary told her about Demeter ascending from the underworld every spring to make the fields flower and the seed corn grow.

'Those are idols,' Miriam said. 'Don't you see that they're idols?'

The next morning, Mary plucked up her courage and asked her teacher, 'Is Demeter an idol?'

He laughed for the first and only time. 'You ought to know better, you who belong to the chosen people with the only just god.'

Mary did not understand, but dared not ask again, and when he saw her surprise, he went on, 'You could say that both Persephone and Demeter are symbols. A symbol is a sign for something that exists in all our lives but cannot be understood.'

Mary was none the wiser, but she did memorize his words.

Like all visitors to the house of pleasure, Erigones was curious about its activities and was attracted to the honey-coloured Serena like a moth to the light. He never neglected any opportunity to greet her and consume her with his eyes, but they never actually spoke, for he was too shy. Serena was flattered and often made excuses to come into the office during lessons, then apologized and went out again challengingly swinging her hips.

Mary was jealous. One day she leaned over toward her teacher and whispered confidentially: 'Serena is a heathen.'

This time her teacher did not laugh. He was angry.

'So am I. So are Leonidas and Euphrosyne and all the others here who are kind to you. According to your religion, everyone in the world is a heathen – Romans, Greeks, Dacians, Syrians, Egyptians, Teutons – all except the Jews. I have no desire to influence you, but I find your Jewish faith loathsome, arrogant and circumscribed.'

Mary found it hard to sleep that night. Erigones' words kept running through her head, and to make things worse, she was ashamed of everything she had not said. About God's alliance with Abraham's seed and about the Holy Scriptures that guided the actions of the faithful. Tomorrow, she thought, or the next day, Leonidas would be coming. I must ask him.

But nothing turned out as she had imagined.

Euphrosyne had hesitated, but had finally pulled herself together and told Miriam that she must return to work, in her own interests, too, she added, for half of what she earned went to herself. 'Your purse is thin. You'll need some capital when you go out into the world again.'

Miriam did not reply or meet her eye. A few hours later, she had disappeared. It was evening and Mary finally did what was forbidden, went to find Euphrosyne in the noisy throng in the main hall. They searched, only the two of them at first, then all the girls who were free, throughout the garden and along the lake. The cook and the gardener were sent into the alleyways in toward town, while the women continued along the shore, searching in every nook and cranny and calling out 'Miriam, Miriam,' so that it echoed across the lake.

At dawn, her body floated ashore in the far north, lacerated by the sharp rocks.

The seven women sat in anguish in the big kitchen, as if for a moment they had seen in the dead woman their own destinies.

Euphrosyne closed the house. There would be no guests that night. Wrapped in her long black cloak, she strode the streets, tired out, trying with little success not to think about Miriam and what she might have done for the girl – tried to find a Jewish foster home, for instance, or spoken to the rabbi in the Jewish quarter, restricted Miriam to cleaning and cooking? But the latter was the only possibility, for a Jewish family would never have accepted spoiled fruit and the rabbi would never speak to a brothel keeper.

I could have put her to sewing, she thought. But the lovely Miriam was much sought after by the clients.

Unknowingly, she had left the Greek sector and was walking toward the Jewish quarter of town. Euphrosyne was usually hardened to the contempt she met in these streets, children shouting insults at her and adults staring, their eyes burning with ill will and greedy curiosity. But today it troubled her, and she turned back toward home. No more Jewish girls, she thought, then the next moment she remembered Mary. Oh well, she was Leonidas' problem.

They buried Miriam the next day beneath the great rose bushes in the garden. At the open grave, Mary read all the prayers she could remember from the synagogue in Magdala, some in Hebrew, others in Aramaic. Sometimes she mixed both languages and words, perhaps even the meaning of the prayers, but her voice was strong and not once did she stumble.

'Who can count the sand of the sea, the drops of the rain and the days of eternity. And the depths of the sea – or of wisdom.

Let us fall into the hand of the Lord, for great as he is, as great is his mercy.'

Erigones was on the outskirts of the little group around the grave, reluctantly impressed by the beautiful words and the clear voice of the child. The last to join the burial guests was Leonidas, who had been away on one of his many assignments when Miriam had died.

When the child had stopped reading over the grave, she turned and bowed slightly, but was so pale, Euphrosyne was worried and tried to silence the wails of the women tearing their hair and weeping out their despair.

But the girl appeared not to hear them. Her eyes unseeing, she walked stiffly through the group of mourners until a call reached her, the voice of Leonidas.

'Mary, Mary.'

Suddenly she was able to run, straight into the arms of the Greek, who lifted her up and put her head against his shoulder. She was as tense as if the blood had ceased flowing through her limbs. 'Dear child, dear child,' was all he said.

He carried her to the room she had shared with Miriam and lay down on the narrow bed with her body close to his own. He was not worried like Euphrosyne, for he had seen many people in shock and knew it seldom took the life of a human being.

'She needs something to drink.'

'I'll bring some hot milk and honey.'

Mary closed her mouth tight as the sweet drink was pressed to her lips.

But Leonidas said, 'Drink now, girl,' and she obeyed. To Euphrosyne he said, 'I'll stay here tonight.'

As Euphrosyne left them, she was thinking what a strange love it was binding those two together, a warrior Greek and a Jewish child. Almost a destiny. One weary wine-soaked night, he had said the child was in some inexplicable way bound to his destiny.

Leonidas slept uncomfortably and spasmodically, but he was

used to that, so it did not trouble him. When they woke toward dawn, he winked at her and said, 'Now we'll have something to eat, just you and me. Then we'll go out into the garden and talk about Miriam.'

She was frightened and at the same time pleased, and she whispered that they must also talk about God.

They crept down to the kitchen, where Leonidas took out bread and yogurt, cheese and salted mutton. Mary watched with wonder as this handsome officer arranged the food.

After they had eaten, they went down to the shore where the great red sun was just appearing behind the hills in the east, its slanting rays colouring the lake and the morning mist slowly rising from the water up toward the town and the mountains.

'Why did she kill herself?'

The brutal question worked just as he had hoped. The words came pouring out of Mary. 'Because she had committed so many sins that God would never forgive her, for she had lived among heathens who worshipped terrible idols and because I came to love Demeter.'

'Demeter?'

Mary told him how she had read the story and how captivated she had been, and how frightened she had been when Miriam had said that the girl who made the spring flowers open and close on the slopes was a heathen goddess, like Isis or Venus, who wallowed in sin among the stars in the heavens.

Leonidas was surprised. 'But Demeter is an image or a saga of the miracle of spring.'

Mary shook her head without understanding. 'Why do you believe it's a woman who makes the earth green? When it's God who does that?'

'It's women who carry life on. If the women weren't fertile and didn't bear children, we would disappear from the face of the earth.'

'Do you believe in many gods?'

'I don't think we should have definite perceptions of what is invisible and immeasurable. But the unknown power in nature and within ourselves may need many images, many expressions. The story of Demeter describes what is incomprehensible in the return of spring and the renewal of life.'

Mary thought hard about what Erigones had said which she had not understood. 'A symbol?'

'Yes.'

'But it says in the scriptures . . .'

'Mary, have you read the scriptures?'

The girl closed her eyes, and when she opened them, they were hard with anger. 'You know nothing about the laws of the Jews,' she said, thinking about the school in Magdala, where her brothers had been allowed to go to once they were five, while she had no right even to ask them what they had learned.

'I don't know whether I've read the laws,' Leonidas said. 'But I've read your Holy Writ.'

'You've read . . . ?'

She was so surprised, she was at a loss for words. She kept shaking her head, but after a while asked him a question. 'You know Hebrew?'

'There's a translation into Greek.'

Leonidas told her about Septuagint, the book seventy wise men had worked on for centuries. But Mary was not interested in the labours of old Jews in distant Alexandria. She wanted to know what Leonidas thought of the Holy Writ.

'It's full of beauty and ancient wisdom,' he said. 'What I liked best was the idea that you serve God by being merciful to your fellow men.'

The child drew a deep sigh of relief.

'Just as in the ancient Greek scripts, there are lots of heroic sagas and amazing adventures. I remember a man who blew a horn so that the walls of Jericho fell. Another hero whose strength was in his hair and who lost it all when a treacherous woman cut it off . . . Do you know these tales?'

Mary nodded. She wanted to say that they were not tales, but what happened when God's strength came into the possession of man. But she said nothing.

Finally, he said: 'I don't think you can put the whole of your destiny into the hands of God. I think everyone bears the responsibility for his or her own decisions. Miriam decided to die. It's difficult to understand, and very sad.'

Mary wept.

Life returned to normal in the house of pleasure. With the help of wine, the girls forgot the terrible thing that had happened. Mary had a pain in her stomach and had to stay in bed. That meant she had time to think, to make comparisons between then and now, between people in the village – the orthodox, and people here – the unclean.

But as she did so, things only grew worse.

9

Mary Magdalene let the scroll lie. She could not find the energy that evening to go through what she had written. Her back was aching and her fingers stiff from writing.

She was cold.

Slowly, she got up and went to close the shutters.

Dusk was creeping into the treetops and it would soon be dark. Leonidas had not yet come home. Perhaps this was one of the nights he would spend with his boy. What had he said that morning?

She could not remember.

She lit the lamps in the kitchen and made a meal for two.

Then she ate hers, washed, and crawled into her warm bed. She stretched, the warmth and relaxation slowly lessening the pain in her back.

Early next morning, she read through what she had written. One question worried her. How old had she been when Leonidas disappeared? Ten? Twelve? She shook her head. She could not remember. Children are so free in their relations to time, she thought.

Toward afternoon, she heard Leonidas coming home, his firm steps up the garden path, the door opening, and his call: 'Mary, Mary, I'm here.'

She went to meet him and at once saw that he was in low spirits. Disappointed? Burdened with guilt? She smiled a little wider than usual and that helped. His bearing softened and he said, 'I'm rather tired.'

She kissed him on the cheek. 'I've been writing about you. Perhaps you'd like to read it while I get the meal?'

'Yes, indeed.'

He went into the library and she gave him the long scroll before returning to the kitchen. While she boiled beans and cooked the fish with freshly picked buds from the caper bushes, she thought about Leonidas' lover, a handsome but heartless boy. He was not good for Leonidas, but there was nothing she could do about that.

Leonidas came back into the kitchen as Mary was laying the table.

'You exaggerate,' he said. 'It just isn't possible for that simple, scarcely thirty-year-old warrior to have had so much wisdom.'

Mary flushed.

'Writing has taught me to respect a child's memories,' she said with some heat. 'Every word of it is probably not true, but it's a child's interpretation of everything that happened and was said.'

'I give in,' said Leonidas, holding up his hand and laughing.

Mary had to smile.

'How old was I when you had to leave?'

His face darkened.

'That was the same year the tribune Titus finally broke our agreement,' he said. 'Then you'd been with Euphrosyne for five years.'

'Oh, Leonidas, I understood so little.'

'Perhaps we should try to remember together. I'll stay at home tomorrow and tell you, while you make notes.'

10

'Something very strange happened to me that night I found you in the mountains. I've never understood it and sometimes I'm prepared to believe, as religious people do, that God intervened in my life.'

Why should he? It had been a dreadful evening.

He fell silent, then smiled.

'I'm sure you think I'm exaggerating,' he said. 'But there was something divine about that child, a light . . . So I wasn't at all surprised when I found you again many years later with that young man of God in Galilee.'

He stopped abruptly. 'Why are you so occupied with your own childhood?' he asked.

'Because I must know who I am. I've had the peculiar idea that if you're to testify to the truth, then you must be true yourself.'

'I'm sure you're right, but you set your sights very high. I've got no further than trying to get used to myself.'

Mary laughed. 'Perhaps that's the same thing. But go on telling me about the evening you found me.'

'I lifted you up and you fainted with terror. I wrapped you in

45

the cloak. Then I rode to Euphrosyne's, the only woman I knew in Tiberias that I had any confidence in. When I left you there, I made plans, foolish and lovely plans. My contract with the Romans would run out in a few years and I would be free to return to Antioch with a small daughter. My whole family would be delighted that I had had a child.'

'You wanted children?'

'That would rehabilitate me, wouldn't it?'

Mary's eyes narrowed and her voice hardened. 'That was why you went to the expense of educating me,' she said. 'Finding a teacher for me and all that?'

He looked at her in surprise, for this was unlike her.

'No,' he said. 'I simply wanted to give you everything I could. And it was already clear when you learned Greek that you had a great gift of understanding. And you were eager to learn, and inquisitive.'

'I'm sorry.'

'There were some worries. A house of pleasure was not a suitable place for a small girl. But I had no choice, and there were few prejudices at Euphrosyne's. I didn't think about there being any religious difficulties at first. It wasn't until Miriam took her own life that I realized what it meant for a Jewish child to live in a "house of sin".'

Another long silence.

'Then I was uneasy about you not wanting to play, that you were such a serious child. I gave you a doll. Do you remember?'

She shook her head. No, she did not.

They sat in silence before Leonidas went on. 'Someone once said that if you want to see eternal life manifesting itself, you should suffer little children and forbid them not, to come unto me.'

Mary's eyes darkened with grief and she heard a voice running through her head . . . 'for such is the kingdom of God.'

They broke off for a simple meal in the kitchen. He was

uneasy. Had he hurt her? She smiled and said self-knowledge was the whole purpose of her striving. Then she tried to explain that there had never been time for play in her childhood, that even small children had to work.

'At least, girls did,' she said. 'My brothers played at warfare and practised killing Romans from the ambush in the mountains.'

'You could hardly call that playing,' said Leonidas bitterly.

They went back to the library.

'At the same time that you began lessons with Erigones, my father died,' he went on. 'I had a long letter from my mother, probably dictated by Livia. In heartrending terms, they appealed to me to come home. I did not grieve for my father. We had never been close. You know, the only son is to take over and be responsible for everything and everyone. From childhood on.

'As a boy, I escaped, disappearing into a world of daydreams of heroes and exploits. And playing at adventures and great deeds. I was an easy victim for the Roman officers looking for people among the Greeks in Antioch to join the legions. So I signed up. I was eighteen and of age. My father never forgave me.'

He sighed.

'I've never regretted it. I saw the world and it was much larger and crueller and more complicated and difficult to make out than I had imagined.'

'You had a letter from your mother?'

'Yes, it came at an opportune moment. I went to Titus, the tribune, who read it and said he understood. And that I had actually fulfilled my contract with the Roman army. So I started completing my reports and began negotiations for your adoption. That was more complicated than I had thought. After all, even a foundling has parents, as the lawyer said. At that stage, I had already found out your father's name, but it was on the list of the Jewish rebels. So I couldn't use that.'

He fell silent, his eyes straying out over Mary's garden.

47

'Then that damned expedition against the Parthians put an end to all my plans. The cohort from Tiberias was taken out, the soldiers jubilant, as they were all tired of the Jews and their treacherous ambushes. The tribune began by flattering me. I was one of his best officers. He couldn't manage without me. My knowledge of the caravan routes through Syria was invaluable. When all the grand talk failed to have any effect, he took to power language, tore up my resignation application, and snapped that the expedition would begin within a week.

'I went to Euphrosyne. But you must remember that moment yourself.'

Yes, she remembered the invulnerable Leonidas sitting on a stool, crying like a child.

'I won't tell you about being captured by those damned Bedouins who ambushed and killed my soldiers in the desert. I presume they were useful years. I had to learn what it meant to be a slave, despised and mocked, whipped when the gentlemen wanted some fun. I was no hero. I was feeble, wept, and begged for mercy, which only increased their pleasure. And I was a poor slave, unused to manual work. They kept me alive because one of them had recognized me as the son of a rich silk merchant in Antioch. The negotiations over the ransom went on for years, but at that time my miserly brother-in-law was head of the merchant house. Then fortunately he died and Livia took over. She almost ruined the firm, paid up, and got me released.'

'Blessed Livia.'

'Yes. But I've done my bit.'

He laughed. 'No one escapes his destiny. I became a silk merchant, just as Father had decided. As far as you're concerned . . .'

The words hung in the air.

'Not until I was going to tell Livia about my daughter in Galilee did it dawn on me that you were now adult. I had to change my words and tell her about a young woman I loved. But that was also true.'

'But not as she believed.'

'No. She wanted nephews and nieces, heirs descended down the family.'

'We share the blame,' said Mary, but Leonidas groaned. She thought about how entangled in lies they were.

'You know the rest,' said Leonidas in a thin voice. 'I went to Rome and signed a very advantageous agreement. My years as a centurion came in useful, as well as my connections and my reputation as a hero. It was said that I had managed to escape from the Parthians, an enemy I had never even seen.

'Yes, by all the gods. Shortly after the trip to Rome, I went back to Palestine, found Euphrosyne, who was on the point of leaving and going back to Corinth. And she told me the incredible story of Jesus of Nazareth.'

The next day, Mary was working alone in the library. As she made a clean copy of her notes, she kept feeling something essential had been said. She looked through the notes and her memories, then stopped at the doll she did not remember, and found words she did not understand.

The children who belonged in the kingdom of heaven, that spontaneous manifestation of life, the joy. Lilies of the field, flowers that praise God by growing and not worrying about the future. Something else Jesus had said the first time she had met him, that spring when the swallows were flying north over their heads, something about the complete trust birds had in the winds.

He never said nature was beautiful.

God is creating now, she thought, at this moment.

That night she dreamt about Quintus, the Roman boy who had taught her at least one game.

I I

A letter came from Leonidas, a cheerful, jolly missive assuring her he would soon be back in Tiberias, but already at first reading she knew he was lying, that he was not only deceiving himself, but also trying to deceive her.

Then nothing.

Euphrosyne went to the new tribune and was received with malicious friendliness and thanked for the orderly and sophisticated way in which she dealt with her activities. It was extremely important for the morale of the soldiers, he told her.

An old man, tired and finished.

Euphrosyne quickly told him about the child she had undertaken to care for on behalf of the centurion Leonidas. Now she wanted to know where Leonidas was.

He looked troubled, called for his scribe, who took out the reports from the Roman expedition to the kingdom of Parthia.

'A total failure of a war,' he said.

She had a strong sense that he had not needed the reports and that he knew, but wanted time. Then he said that an advance troop led by Leonidas had been wiped out in an ambush. The Romans had counted their dead, but the centurion was not among them. There was a possibility that he had been taken prisoner, but . . .'

'But?'

'The Parthians don't usually take prisoners.'

Euphrosyne took a long detour through the new settlers' part of the town, streets where it was difficult to make your way among the building sites and heaps of bricks. She was miserable, weighed down with her responsibility for Mary.

What should she do?

She stopped to watch four workmen fitting a beautifully carved door into one of the new houses and by the time the heavy door was in place, she had made up her mind. She would look on the girl as her daughter. Mary would be Greek. Euphrosyne would wind down her activities. Then she would return to Corinth with her daughter. And a handsome fortune in good Roman coins. But now it was a matter of telling Mary. No lying, and yet being considerate. It turned out to be simpler than she had feared. Mary had only to meet Euphrosyne's eyes and in both of them was certainty and despair.

'He's dead?'

'They don't know. His body wasn't among the dead.'

'Prisoner?'

'The tribune said the Parthians don't usually take prisoners.' Mary was dry eyed and rigid.

And it stayed that way, unapproachable with either consolation or friendliness. All words came up against a wall she had raised between herself and others.

'If only she would at least cry,' the girls in the house kept saying. 'If only she . . .'

She must be kept busy before she turns in on herself completely, thought Euphrosyne. She set Mary to sewing, but the girl's fingers were too impatient for the needle and the work of mending tunics and darning mantles was not productive. Not even embroidery pleased her, despite the bright colours and beautiful flowers.

Then one day Mary took to her bed. 'I've a pain in my stomach,' she whispered.

Euphrosyne left her there, but returned an hour or two later and just sat at her bedside.

'Dear child,' she kept saying. 'Dear child.'

It was so unusual for Euphrosyne to be emotional that her words got through the wall.

'Why does everyone forsake me?' Mary cried out.

'Not everyone,' said Euphrosyne, and Mary could hear she was angry. 'I am here, and I am doing what I can.'

51

Then she left the room.

Mary stayed there, thinking how difficult it all was, for there was no reason why Euphrosyne should give her food and houseroom, friendship, and care. No money was coming from Leonidas any longer and she was of no use in the house. Why not throw her out on the streets with the other beggar children?

She was ashamed.

Then it struck her that Euphrosyne was counting on her, as a whore.

They said she was pretty.

Dear Lord, help me.

She thought about Miriam and now she understood.

She leaped out of bed, pulled on her tunic and ran downstairs straight into Euphrosyne's office, where as usual she was sitting over her accounts.

'I won't be a whore,' she cried.

'Nor is that included in my plans,' Euphrosyne said, coldly, but then suddenly her voice broke. To her immense surprise, Mary saw that she was crying. It was so terrible and unbelievable that it broke down the wall around her and she gave way to her grief, a wail rising in her throat and the tears overflowing.

But nothing could allay Euphrosyne's bitterness.

'You're an ungrateful creature,' she said. 'Go to your room and be ashamed. Think about Leonidas and his loyalty. And mine. You clearly don't even know what love is.'

The next day, Euphrosyne said that Mary was to put things right by going and helping in the kitchen. Learning to cook was an art a woman would always have use for.

Things went better for Mary there, partly because ever since she had come to the house, she had liked the cook. He had been given the handsome name of Octavianus, but he was actually a cheerful Gaul who loved food, Euphrosyne, and life in this house of pleasure.

He called her his assistant, taught her how to trim and brown a roast, gut a fish and fry it golden brown, render vegetable stock into bouillon, and how to make sauces, as well as teaching her the thousand secrets of herbs and spices. He encouraged her, occasionally praising her, but he often shook his head.

'You lack what is most important,' he said. 'And that's the actual joy in it.'

She was very tired by the evenings, her body from all the hard work, her head from all that was new. But before she fell asleep, she wondered about what Octavianus had said about her lacking joy.

She lacked love, too, Euphrosyne had said, but she had plenty of shame. Dear Lord, how ashamed she was.

A day or so later, she was summoned to Euphrosyne's office. She went as she was, in her coarse tunic, stained with blood and spots of fat, and stood stiffly in the doorway, thinking that she must somehow say it.

'Can you forgive me?'

'I have to apologize myself,' said Euphrosyne, flushing. 'I used hard words. And unjust.'

'No,' said the girl calmly. 'I think you were right.'

Euphrosyne looked at Mary. She was quite tall now, but was still painfully thin, her face hollowed like a sculpture that had stood out in fierce winds and lashing rain for far too long.

'Listen, Mary. We must have a talk at another time, but at the moment I have something to tell you. Sit down, will you.'

Mary brushed down her tunic and sat on the very edge of the stool.

'When I heard from the tribune to say that Leonidas . . . was missing, I made a decision. I decided I would regard you as my daughter. In a few years, I am going to sell this house and go back with you to Corinth.'

Mary's eyes narrowed with the effort to understand. 'Your daughter?' she said finally. 'Do you want me as your child?'

'Yes.'

53

'You want me to be your child?'

'Yes.'

Mary got up, her legs weak. 'Why?' she whispered.

'Because I'm fond of you, of course.' Euphrosyne's answer was brief, her voice gruff.

'I hurt so.'

Mary was hugging her stomach with both hands and Euphrosyne told her to go straight to her room and lie down. 'I'll get the doctor and you can be properly examined. And get better.'

Mary lay very still in bed as the doctor squeezed her and said to Euphrosyne, 'I don't think she's ill, but she's under-nourished and dehydrated.'

I should have noticed, Euphrosyne thought. Then she was angry and found an outlet by summoning the cook and shouting and him. 'How can you cook food with a child who is starving to death!'

Octavianus looked at the girl on the bed. 'She finds no joy in food.'

'Then you must make sure she does,' cried Euphrosyne in fury, though aware she was being unjust.

But the doctor stopped her, turned to the cook and said: 'You must now take the responsibility of making sure the girl eats so that she becomes nice and plump. You're a master of good food. Make delicious little dishes and sit at table with her while she eats. I rely on you.'

Mary was made to drink a whole goblet of honey-milk, and when she tasted the bitterness through the sweetness, she knew she would be able to sleep, and for a long time.

Euphrosyne tucked her in and sat beside her for a while. As she rose to go, Mary said, 'You see, I've never had anyone to be like.'

12

Mary Magdalene decided to spend the day working in her garden in Antioch. She went up the narrow steps that wound their way between the terraces, and when she came to her herb garden, she saw to her satisfaction that her plants were shooting as they should in early spring.

The garden was high up, so high that on a clear day like this, she could see right over the town wall and make out the sea in the west.

She stood there with the pruning knife and hoe in her hands as she gazed for a long time out over the sea, a streak of brilliant blue from horizon to horizon, a sail here and there, signs of mankind in the infinity.

She remembered the first time she had ever seen the sea, when Leonidas had been searching for her and had found her in Galilee, where she had walked, confused and mad, obsessed by the desire to see Jesus. Here by the blue sea, his spirit must surely be found and once again show himself to her.

She had looked like a beggar woman and was one, begging her bread at people's doors, asking for houseroom, and sometimes being allowed to stay overnight in an outhouse with the animals, though she mostly slept under the open sky.

It was a hot summer.

No one had recognized her.

According to ancient custom, she had strewn ash in her hair and, mixed with sweat, it had run in rivulets down her face. She never washed and grew used to the smell from her body. Her monthly bleeding came and she let it run down her legs. Her skin was dry and cracked, burnt by the sun and covered with sores.

The night before Leonidas found her, she was sleeping under an upturned boat on the shore and had a dream in which she was walking over land in an unfamiliar landscape, asking everyone she met for the sea. Most just shook their heads, but a few pointed in a certain direction, so she followed their instructions, but never found the sea.

Once she saw some waters that seemed to have no end. It became a long and exhausting walk to get there, but she was driven by her longing and hopes. When she finally reached the shore, to her despair she saw that it was a stretch of river she had seen and thought had no end. She tried imagining the waters of the river were like her, on their way to the sea, but was unable to follow the winding course, so she stopped by the trees on the riverbank, a place she knew, but where people no longer lived.

She wept with despair in her sleep.

It was strange that he recognized her. His cry of 'Mary, Mary' reached her in the morning as she rolled out from under the boat. But she found she could neither answer nor even raise a hand in greeting.

I thought I was dead, she thought. But I was stark staring mad.

He took her to a house he had borrowed, put her in a warm bath, washed her hair and rinsed it again and again, then soaked the scabs off the sores on her body.

She submitted like an infant, but her blue eyes followed him, grave and questioning. By the time he had finally dried her, massaging her with a large towel and rubbing ointment on the open sores, she was able to ask, 'Leonidas, do you think I'm sick in my head?'

'You've probably been a little, but you'll soon be well again.'

She could hear he was frightened.

He made her eat.

Before she fell asleep, he said, 'As soon as you're better, we'll go to the sea.'

They went by wagon. To the Roman soldiers controlling all vehicles, he said: 'My wife has been ill. We're on our way to the sea, where she is to rest.'

They looked with pity at Mary's scorched face and thin body, glanced through Leonidas' papers and politely waved them on, Mary scarcely conscious of what was going on. It wasn't until she stood by the endless sea, bluer than the sky, but closer and full of strength, that she found her way back to herself and tried to explain: 'Since last time you left . . .'

'I know,' he said. 'As soon as I got back I heard about it. That damned Pilate had Jesus crucified. I had a feeling he was threatened. I oughtn't to have left him.'

Leonidas was also in despair.

'You couldn't have done anything. He decided himself.'

'So incomprehensible!'

'Yes, no one will ever understand.'

They had seven days to talk about what had happened, but what she remembered most of all of their time on the shore outside Caesarea was the waves breaking day and night, great waves that washed her until she was empty.

Mary brushed her memories aside. It was all so long ago now.

She got down on her hands and knees and started pulling up the weeds. She noticed the soil was drier than usual at this time of year and that was worrying. She would have to start watering soon and she sighed even now at the thought of the heavy work of carrying water up to the top terraces.

As she was resting and slaking her thirst from the water jar, she noticed the mist sweeping in over the sea. The blue colour had gone and she now had to be content with looking at her house, the lovely house Leonidas had had built on the slope.

She began wondering how it had come about that they had ended up here. Neither of them had wanted to live in the seething noisy town, that was clear. But why just here, on the outskirts of the Jewish quarter?

The finger of God, she thought, but she smiled. Perhaps it was

Leonidas wanting to give her a home close to Jewish fellow believers.

The thought made her laugh.

Then she thought perhaps it had been for her.

A long time had gone by before she had dared go to the synagogue, slipping in to the women's gallery to hear Rabbi Amasya speaking. She listened in wonder to the words she recognized, about the God you could only serve by being merciful.

Rabbi Amasya told an old story about a Greek who went to the rabbi and asked to be instructed in the Torah. He was given the answer that it was simple, that all of Jewish wisdom could be found in a single rule: Love your neighbour as yourself.

Amasya quoted the prophets: Hosea who listened to God and heard him say, 'For I have delight in love and not in sacrifice.' And not without pride, he said that Judaism was the first religion to preach responsibility for all fellow human beings. He spoke of Amos, the prophet for whom Jehovah spoke on behalf of the oppressed. People may close their eyes to injustices and cruelty to the poor, but God did not.

The rabbi quoted from the scriptures: 'Therefore all things whatsoever you would that men should do to you, do you even so to them.'

Mary heard another voice, a young voice saying: 'All that you wish people to do to you, shall you do for them.'

She was far away in the unusual light over the hills by the blue sea when the service ended in a prayer to God who was beyond our understanding, but was on the side of the powerless and the despairing. As the women around her rose to leave, Mary looked at the rabbi down there, her gaze so strong that he looked up, met her eyes, and smiled. As she left the synagogue the last of all, he was standing in the doorway.

'I knew Leonidas' wife was a Jewess,' he said. 'So I have waited a long time for you.'

'I'll be back.'

On the following Sabbath, the rabbi told another story.

A man died, was wrapped in a shroud and placed in a coffin. Many people assembled for his burial, mourning and weeping.

But the man was in suspended animation and was awakened by the wailing. He banged on the coffin lid.

Horrified, the mourners looked at each other. But the bravest of them opened the coffin, saw the dead man sit up and heard him cry out, 'I am not dead.'

At which the brave man said in a firm voice: 'Both the priest and the doctor have pronounced you dead. So lie down again.'

Then they nailed down the coffin again and lowered it into the grave.

A murmur ran through the great hall, and an astonished titter or two, but Mary's laughter filled the synagogue. Heads turned and necks craned toward the women's gallery. Appalled, she slapped her hand to her mouth, but she noticed the rabbi smiling slightly, and that he gave her a grateful look.

The very next day, Rabbi Amasya knocked on her door. Leonidas received him and told him he had listened to his wife's account of the services at the synagogue.

'You must be a brave man.'

'Antioch is a large town and most Jews here have for generations been influenced by Greek thinking. There are shifting perceptions here, Gnostic Jews and the new Christians. So we have many seekers from other religions. And people who are just curious.'

'But what do the orthodox say?'

'They're probably disappointed. There are always people who are so full of fears, they have to stay within the authority of the rules.'

Leonidas laughed.

It became the start of a warm friendship.

Mary got up from her weeding and stretched, surprised by all the memories that had washed over her that day. Must be all this writing, she said to herself. As if sluice gates had been opened.

The next moment she heard the dry rustle in the bushes that told her that rain was coming. The mist from the sea had met the heat from the earth and had turned into heavy clouds. Although she ran down the steps, she was soaked through by the time she reached the house.

The sea sent yet more rain over Antioch when Mary was to sleep that night. She heard it striking the stone-laid courtyard and rustling through the tops of the fig trees.

Blessed, she thought.

It had been a good day.

Tomorrow she would return to that thirteen-year-old in Tiberias.

13

The cook took very seriously his task of persuading Mary to eat. He created delicious dishes that gave off exciting aromas and glowed in lovely colours. Then he sat down opposite her and watched every spoonful going to her mouth. When things went slowly and she stopped, he resorted to blackmail.

'You hold my destiny in your hands,' he said, and as Mary snorted, he went on in a trembling voice. 'Don't you see, if you don't eat and get better, Euphrosyne will sell me on the slave market. Can you take the responsibility for that?'

After a dramatic silence, he managed to make his eyes fill with tears before digressing into voluble descriptions of the horrible fates ahead of him. He would be flogged and humiliated by a grim Roman matron and he would be made to cook barbaric food.

'Did you know the Romans eat snakes? And pelicans with fish sauce!' he shuddered.

Then he almost wept as he described how he would have to spend his nights in a sooty corner of that Roman kitchen, bitten by dogs and kicked by all the other slaves in the house.

Mary was profoundly moved, obediently chewed the food, and swallowed.

But the next time he started on the story of the terrifying future ahead of him, she had had time to think, and she told him that Euphrosyne had a warm heart and would never sell her cook, a man she liked and greatly valued.

'You're more childish than I thought,' said Octavianus, his dark eyes glowing like burning charcoal as he went on.

'Euphrosyne has a heart of ice. Didn't you know she has never loved anyone before? Now she's fond of you and the gods alone know how it will end.'

Long silence again, then that terrible question. 'What happens when a heart of ice melts?'

Mary was struck dumb. But she could see it, a lump of ice in a breast suddenly beginning to trickle away. 'I don't know,' she whispered.

'No, you see? No one can imagine that. I lie awake at night wondering about it.'

Out of sheer terror, Mary ate up every crumb on her plate. That gave her a stomach ache, so she had to run to the privy, and as she sat there, she felt an unexpected joy. That afternoon, she knocked on Euphrosyne's office door.

'Have you got a heart of ice?'

Euphrosyne smiled her strange unsmiling smile. 'Like everyone else, I have a heart of flesh and blood,' she said.

'I thought so,' said Mary, and then she dared do the unheard of – she threw herself into Euphrosyne's arms and hugged her. Euphrosyne flushed with delight and held tightly on to the girl.

'I hear you're eating as you should,' she said. 'Your cheeks are getting rounder, but you're still very pale. We must try some fresh air. When you were small, you always liked helping Setonius in the garden.'

'I'd love to do that.'

Setonius had always liked the child for her gravity and the unerring feeling in those fingers for every tender root as she weeded around the plants and roses. But now she was almost adult.

He soon found that she had not severed her link with what could not be spoken. She knew flowers had thoughtful dispositions, and that no plant was as unaffected as it pretended to be. She said she loved the old trees down on the edge of the lake, simply consuming time. In that way, she considered, they made time cease.

She had gone on asking questions, as children do, not like adults, who are seldom prepared to listen to the answers. That was how she came to hear so many stories.

He had a story for every plant in the big garden.

The day she arrived to be a gardener's labourer, he was just about to cut open the fruits of the sycamore. He showed her how the flowers grew inside the fruit, hidden from the outside world. Like the foetus in the womb, he said, and he told her that the sycamore was the tree of the Egyptian goddess of love. Her name was Hathor, and she helped everyone secretly suffering from unhappy love.

Then he sliced into every fruit to drive out the insects trying to lay their eggs inside the hidden flowers. Mary thought it endless labour, and messy. But she climbed the ladder and soon learned how to make the cut correctly and a few sweaty hours later, the fruits were freed of their intruders.

'In six days, you'll see,' he said. 'Now we've helped Hathor, and soon she'll reward us with fruit as golden and sweet as the cheeks of the goddess.'

He smiled at her, but as they washed at the well, he noticed a small worried frown.

'Do you believe in lots of gods?' she asked him as they took a rest in the shade of the great terebinth.

As he did not understand what she meant, he began to tell her about his childhood on a windy island in the Ionian Sea.

'In our village, we had a wealth of gods,' he said, his voice warm with melancholy and longing. 'There was Apollo, as beautiful and strong as the light over the sea. In the fields in spring, we sang hymns to Demeter and thanked her for her fecundity. At the grape harvest, we held feasts in honour of Diosynsus and we danced like madmen.

'A fantastic feast,' he said, smiling at the memory.

'We had a mountain with a view over the endless blue sea,' Setonius went on. 'We had raised a statue of Zeus there. On the edge of the great forest was Artemis, the many-breasted maiden queen. I loved her most of all.'

He blushed as he remembered how the many-breasted goddess had enriched his fantasies.

'You asked about beliefs,' he said. 'But I don't understand you. All these beings were there in nature and made our dreams understandable.'

He fell silent and they listened to the thrush singing at the top of the terebinth tree.

'It was a practical religion, too,' he went on. 'Every god and goddess had his or her field of responsibility. Seamen had to appease the god of the sea, and they did that in the rocky cave by the harbour, where Poseidon resided. The peasants worshipped Demeter before sowing, and the women went to Aphrodite when they were in love. They all considered they had been helped. Greek islanders are a sensible people. They have to be to survive.'

Mary spent the whole afternoon on her knees, weeding the herb beds until Setonius came and stopped her.

'Up you get and take a run before your legs stiffen,' he said. She got up and trotted off, but he laughed at her. 'Run,' he said again. 'You're as young and beautiful as Aphrodite and you should fly over the ground.'

She laughed, too, but she learned eventually, at least so that she felt she were flying, as if her feet were scarcely touching the grass. Euphrosyne came to see what they were doing, and said quietly to Setonius that this was just what the girl needed.

A little later, Octavianus brought their meal in a basket, and for the first time since Leonidas had disappeared, Mary was hungry and devoured the food.

Everything might have gone well. Mary was always to remember with pleasure the years when she was between thirteen and fifteen. Euphrosyne's plans became firmer as she reduced her activities with the aim of leaving altogether, then she would go back to Corinth with Mary, the two slaves and the two oldest courtesans.

But then Mary fell in love.

14

Quintus.

It began quite innocently, the eighteen-year-old Roman a new guest at the pleasure house one evening, and he was terrified. Euphrosyne noticed the symptoms. She had seen them before. The boy was frightened of women as well as of this adventure that had filled his feverish fantasies for so long. Timid and ashamed, he retreated further and further away from the wine and laughter and talk in the main hall, then turned scarlet when a friend laughed at him, making him want to spew. So he headed for the privy, but too late, and turned his stomach inside out just outside the kitchen. As he wiped the sweat off his forehead, his eyes fell on a girl in the light in the kitchen. Never before had he seen a more beautiful sight.

A goddess with long golden hair, standing there chopping an onion.

Was she a slave? No, that was not possible.

Quintus stood stock still for what was perhaps an hour. The girl looked up once and for the first time he saw those amazing eyes, blue eyes, bluer than the sky on a summer's day.

He was now so cold he was shaking. He had to meet her and find out who she was. And he was in luck. The door at the side of the house led straight into the kitchen. He tried opening it without making a sound, but it screeched like an affronted cat and a large man in a chef's cap spun around.

'What do you require, sir?' he said. 'This is no place for the guests of the house.'

Quintus was about to tell a lie and say he had lost his way, but found he could not.

'You smell of vomit, sir,' said the cook. 'You may wash in the bath out here if you like.'

Those amazing blue eyes were now gazing at him, and in his confusion, he wondered how eyes that are light blue could be so profound.

She was laughing at him.

He was ashamed.

In the bath, he washed his face and hands rather unsuccessfully and tried to rub the stains off his toga.

But he found the courage to go back to the kitchen. 'I just wish to apologize,' he stammered.

'That's all right,' said the cook, then eased him over toward the door and out into the garden.

Quintus again took his courage in his hands and whispered, 'Who is she?'

The cook smiled, shook his head and put him right. 'She's Euphrosyne's daughter and not for sale.'

When Octavianus went back into the kitchen, he shrugged his shoulders. 'Idiot,' he said.

'But he was handsome,' said Mary.

'Handsome! A drunk smelling of vomit.'

Quintus was back again early the very next morning. The house was asleep, closed and locked. He slipped along the outer wall, following it as it swung down toward the lake. Down on the shore, he climbed over the wall and found a hiding place in among some prickly bushes. It was an unusually big garden, well kept and blooming. But it was also asleep, only the birds awake. Quintus was cold and gabbled some prayers to Venus, then to his great surprise found that she must have been listening. The girl from yesterday was coming straight across the grass toward him.

What should he do?

She stopped a few steps away from him, picked up a rake and started to work. He dared not even breathe, but his heart was beating so that she must have been able to hear it.

That seemed to be true, too, for the girl suddenly looked straight at him, surprised but unafraid. 'It's only me,' he said.

'I can see that,' said Mary. 'What are you doing here?'

'Up to now, I've only been praying to the gods that you would come.'

'They appear to have been favourably disposed,' she said, her laughter ringing over the garden and silencing the surprised birds.

Setonius then appeared, rather slowly and stiffly, as always early in the mornings. 'So you've started already, Mary,' he said, yawning.

'Yes. And can you guess what my rake found?'

Setonius was not inclined to mysteries at that time of day so he just crossly shook his head. 'A Roman soldier fallen off the wall.'

Setonius woke with a start, strode forward, and took a long look at Quintus. Then he started laughing. 'I'd very much like to know how you fell off the wall,' he said, and his laughter spread along the gravelled paths. Then he examined the boy more closely and decided that despite his confused expression, he seemed quite pleasant.

'I was young once myself,' he said at last. 'So I know what it feels like when your body burns. Mary is beautiful, indeed, but we can't have randy tomcats running around here, which I'm sure you understand. If your intentions are honourable, you must go to her mother and politely ask to be allowed to meet her.'

Quintus bowed and straightened up. 'I'll do that,' he said.

'Good, now please leave the way you came.'

Quintus climbed back over the wall, stopping at the top to wave to Mary. 'We'll meet again,' he said.

'We'll see,' said Mary, but he could see she was not as indifferent as she was pretending to be.

Quintus was on guard duty until the eleventh hour. He marched to and fro, rehearsing in time with his footsteps the words he would say when he spoke to Euphrosyne. She was a stately lady and even the night before, he had been frightened of her.

'My name is Quintus Petronius. I am the son of the centurion Gallus Petronius of the Sixth Legion in Syria. My mother and my sisters live in Rome. We are not rich but we manage. I have come to ask for the hand of Miss Mary.'

The whole speech was soon firmly fixed in his mind as if nailed there.

Yet his mouth was so dry, he was unable to get a word out as he bowed to Euphrosyne. As usual in the afternoon, she was in her office counting her takings with some satisfaction. She nodded in a friendly way. 'And what do you want, good soldier?' she said.

Not a word came from him, so she was forced to go on before the silence became painful.

'I've heard from both my cook and my gardener that you seem to have a strange tendency to fall through rear entrances, through kitchen doors and over walls.'

The corners of her mouth twitched, and he was suddenly made aware of the comical side of everything he had done. He flung out his arms and attempted a laugh. 'I'm not in the habit of behaving like an idiot,' he said.

'Then I hope it won't happen again. As far as Mary is concerned, she is a decent girl. If you wish to meet her and she agrees, then it would be all right if you paid a visit.'

He fell to his knees, flung out his arms and at last managed to get out the rehearsed words.

He's as theatrical as Octavianus, thought Euphrosyne, who couldn't help laughing, which she noticed made him feel he had been slapped, so she pulled herself together.

'It is good that Quintus Petronius has honourable intentions,' she said. 'But before you start talking about marriage, perhaps you should get to know each other, or . . . ?'

'I have known her through a thousand lives,' said Quintus, who had been brought up in the spirit of Plato. But that had no effect, for Euphrosyne did not believe in transmigration.

'Everyone who falls in love becomes a trifle mad,' she said. 'Do not worry, soldier. It will pass.'

'Never,' said Quintus, so convincingly she almost believed him.

She was looking stern as she went ahead of him into the garden where Mary was working in a drift of flowering crocuses as golden as her hair. She was wearing a thin tunic, a new one as far as Euphrosyne could remember, and as blue as her eyes and the sea glittering in the background.

Disquieting signs, Euphrosyne thought. 'Mary,' she said aloud.

'I have come to introduce you to a young man who is burning to be introduced to you. But you yourself must decide.'

Quintus was once again quite speechless.

'As you see,' Euphrosyne went on. 'He is not exactly voluble, and to be honest, nor does he appear to be particularly gifted.'

She knew at that moment that it had been a stupid thing to say, but she was amused by the solemnity of the boy and the girl's expectations. 'The young idiot,' she went on angrily, 'goes by the name of Quintus Petronius and has come to ask for your hand.'

She snorted audibly before continuing. 'I have said he may speak to you, but only if Setonius is present.'

She turned to Setonius. 'You are responsible,' she said, 'for the honour of my daughter.'

Then she turned on her heel and went back to her office with an unpleasant feeling that she had already lost the battle. She had seen it in Setonius' eyes and there was no one's judgment she relied on more than her gardener's.

Mary was far away from her stepmother's disapproval, and took Quintus' hand in hers. 'Perhaps you'd like to see our garden?'

He had grown up in an alley in Rome and was not interested in flowers. Yet he brightened with anticipation and tried to pay attention as she showed him the flower beds and told him about the flowers, shrubs, and trees. But he saw nothing but her and was listening to nothing but that light girlish voice.

'Look at our oleanders,' she said. 'They're an unusual variety and they'll soon have a thousand pink flowers.'

He looked at the prickly bush and had never been happier.

But time was flying and the cook intervened, feeling far greater responsibility for the course of events than Setonius did. He sought them out and briskly pointed out to the young couple that the evening meal was served and the visit over.

'Tomorrow,' said Quintus.

'Yes, tomorrow.'

'There's not much we can do,' Setonius told Euphrosyne.

'Probably not,' she admitted.

He appeared every afternoon at exactly the eleventh hour. Euphrosyne's courtesans fluttered around him like butterflies – 'such a sweet boy, such a sweet little boy.'

'They're only teasing,' said Mary comfortingly. 'Come on, and I'll show you my secret grotto.'

The women's chatter rose – 'So you've got a grotto, have you, Mary, a grotto, a secret cave? . . .'

Peals of laughter.

Neither Mary nor Quintus could make out what was so funny.

The cave was as round as a blown egg, the walls polished over the centuries by the waves as they surged in on stormy nights. Setonius used to dry herbs and spices in it, so it smelled of thyme and rosemary.

The light was soft, a shadowy twilight, and it was quiet, too, the only sound that of the gentle waves as they broke on the rocks. Best of all, the opening of the cave faced the sea, so no one could see them.

Holding hands, they sank on to the soft bed of leaves, and then, neither of them knowing who began and where it would end, they started kissing. Mary, that sensible earthbound creature, lost her head. What is happening to me, what is happening? But when she whispered those words into his ear, he became guarded and withdrew.

'Mary, we must stop.'

'Why?'

'Because soon we won't be able to. Let's sit on the rocks and talk.'

Once up on the rocky ledge above the lake where everyone could see them but no one could hear what they were saying, he began to talk. Now he had a thousand words for his love. He had dreamed about her for many years, but had never dared hope he would ever meet her.

When he had seen her in the kitchen that evening, he had almost fainted, and kept telling himself it could not be possible, he was seeing sights, he was dreaming.

'I was drunk,' he said, and she smiled indulgently, her mind on his mouth, how finely sculpted it was, and how sensitively it reflected every shift of his emotions. Then he repeated what he had said to Euphrosyne, that they had known each other through a thousand lives; they had met, loved, and been parted by cruel fate. Didn't she feel that? Had she forgotten?

Mary was far too busy studying the shell of his ear, the most perfect she had ever seen. She leaned over to whisper something into it, but kissed and bit it instead.

'Mary, we're losing control.'

'I lost control long ago. To be more precise, an hour ago.'

'Setonius,' he said. 'Euphrosyne.'

She nodded. She understood.

But then she felt the pull in her loins, a tension greater than she had ever felt just before her menstruation. That was when it dawned on her what the girls had been laughing about, what had been so very funny in that talk about a secret cave.

Then the cook was suddenly down below, calling out that the evening meal was served.

'Maybe you can eat with us,' Mary whispered as they climbed down.

'No,' he said, terrified at the thought of all those cheerful courtesans. 'I'll come back tomorrow.'

Mary managed to have a moment alone with Euphrosyne after the meal. 'I can't resist it.'

'Then you'll have to give in, won't you?' said Euphrosyne crossly.

The next moment she regretted what she had said, and ran

after the fleeing girl. But Mary had disappeared and the house had begun to fill up with the evening's guests.

A violent squabble broke out in the kitchen that evening. Octavianus threw frying pans onto the stove so that the hot oil spattered, broke eggs with a crash as if they were stones, and yelled at Setonius that he would hit him with a meat cleaver if for one single moment he let those two young idiots go to the cave.

'It's your responsibility,' he shouted.

Setonius tried to say that no one can fight against his destiny, but the cook just shouted that he, Octavianus, was both able to and had to. Also, that he hated all those damned Greeks for their damned belief in destiny.

'A randy soldier and a flattered young girl – what kind of destiny is that?'

Mary was a child, and if he had any say in it, he would lock her up. Until she came to her senses. 'She's spoiled. She's not been thrashed enough,' he shouted.

Setonius looked unhappy. Neither of them noticed the girl hiding behind the kitchen door.

Uneasily.

For a while she tried hating the dramatic cook, but in vain. Then she tried to think about Quintus, and her breasts ached and again she felt that pull below.

The two young people walked along the shore the next few days, whenever they were not sitting fully visible on the rocky ledge. One day, he talked about God, the foolish tribal god of the Jews. He quoted a Roman philosopher who had rewritten the beginning of the scriptures of the Jews. 'In the beginning the Jews created God and made him into their image.'

Quintus laughed, not noticing that Mary was not amused. But he agreed with her when she said the same could be said of all gods.

He mostly talked about his dreams, about his great love for her and the golden future awaiting them.

Mary said nothing most of the time, hugging herself and her secrets to herself. He neither asked, nor saw, that she was beginning to be bored.

He spent a whole afternoon telling her about his family, his mother, a Jewess who enthusiastically worshipped the awful Jewish God.

'She has a word from the scriptures for every occasion,' Quintus said with a scornful laugh.

'But what does your father say?'

'He's hardly ever at home. But he has forbidden her to turn me into a Jew.'

'But your sisters?'

'I don't know them,' he said. 'They live their own life at home, humble and versed in the scriptures, they are, too.'

Mary listened, refusing to let herself be distracted by his mouth or ears, nor even by the brown eyes or the enchanting fringe that kept falling over his forehead.

She could see it all before her, the sisters turned into shadows, the mother's silent power, that maternal power partly exercised with quotes from the scriptures.

Everything in her said no.

'What do you think your mother will say when you have to tell her you found your bride in a brothel?' she said aloud.

He did not reply, and that was answer enough.

She was not even saddened. She glanced at him, wondering for a moment whether he understood that his fragile dreams had just collapsed. She herself had not been dreaming, but simply suffering from thirst. And she was to slake her thirst, Euphrosyne herself had advised her to.

'You can come tonight. Jump over the wall and go to the cave. I'll meet you there as soon as I can get away.'

The moon was full as Mary slipped out through the garden, down to the shore, and up to the grotto where he was waiting. They kissed until they were out of their minds, and Mary gave in, her desire filling mouth and back, thigh, and breast. It hurt when he drove into her and she screamed with pleasure and pain. By all the gods, she did not want to live without this.

They slept for a while, a heavenly sleep. Then she had to wake him. 'You must go now, Quintus. And don't come back, ever.'

The next day, Mary told Euphrosyne that she had done as Euphrosyne had said, and he wouldn't be coming back.

'That was all his love was worth then?' said Euphrosyne.

'Precisely. But it was a wonderful moment, and I've no intention of forgoing it in the future.'

'Mary, I don't want that.'

'But I do.'

The girl had grown up.

She liked men, their purposeful striving to achieve pleasure, and their bodies, nearly always so tense and hard. She learned a lot and always had the courage to show how she wanted it – she was both inventive and demanding. One of the courtesans taught her how to give massage and she found her hands could make men weep. That was not difficult. After intercourse, people are sad.

Her clients were carefully selected by Euphrosyne, primarily Roman and Greek officers.

Occasionally she received a Jewish man. His body was softer but afterward always turned rigid with remorse. Then she was unable to help him and the burning hatred in his eyes frightened her.

Mary talked to Euphrosyne about it, and she said she gave a great deal of thought to the Jewish God who never forgave the sins that he himself decided people should commit.

But she also said she liked the Jews for their high ideals and firm attitudes to life and because many of them showed compassion.

Then she sighed. 'They suffer from eternal feelings of guilt.

74

Their obedience to the laws and acts of goodness never seem to be enough.'

15

Mary Magdalene sat at her writing table in Antioch reading with some surprise her story about how at her own request she became a whore.

Truth always has a forgotten side to it. She had seldom given Quintus a moment's thought and she had totally obliterated her conversation with Euphrosyne.

But when she had been writing the day before, she had put pressure on her memory to an extreme, and had found a lusting adolescent and a foolish passion.

A boy happened to pass by. And as her story had shown, the boy had lit a fire in her blood. Some fuel must already have existed. Perhaps she had never been an innocent fifteen-year-old?

Had eroticism been built into the walls of the house of pleasure? So that she had breathed it in with the air? Or do the bodies of all young girls burn?

In that case, the question remained why most managed to resist and keep their virginity? The answer is obvious – strong taboos existed in their upbringing. In hers? She suddenly remembered the words she had once spoken to Euphrosyne – I have never had anyone to be like. Does that mean I am amoral?

Was that what Jesus had meant when he said she was one of the innocents?

She now lived a celibate life with a man she loved as a brother. The desires of the body, where had they gone?

She smiled slightly, for she could certainly feel them in fleeting moments, as when she occasionally met the Jewish rabbi in private.

He was a lovely man and they never dared even look at each other. He had lovely hands, as tempting as Quintus' ear had once been.

But she no longer burned like fire. She regarded her body's reaction almost with amusement, the blood hot in her veins, the tension in her breasts, the pull of her loins.

She had put a distance between herself and her desires. Like Euphrosyne, Mary thought she would write a letter to her stepmother and yet again try to persuade Leonidas to go to Corinth. A voyage. They could set sail when the heat of the summer was over.

16

Cool came on the wind from the sea, as usual in the afternoons in Antioch. It had been a hot day and Mary went out to water the garden.

She sighed as she looked over her flower beds. No flowers smiled at her, no vetches or mignonettes, carnations or toadflax had survived their six-month life and were now, dry and dead, rustling in the wind.

It looked untidy.

But the time to cut them all down had not come, for the seeds, almost invisibly small and enclosed in their watertight shells, were still drilling their way down into the scorched soil.

Some moisture would help, Mary thought, and filled another can.

The irises and cyclamens also looked dead, but she confidently gave their tubers a good soaking so they would survive even this summer and flower again after the winter rains. One single flower, dried to tissue paper, still glowed blue among the irises to tell her that her eyes were the same colour.

When Mary went to the well to fetch another can of water, the winds swept down from the upper terraces, bringing with them the scent of oil-rich shrubs, thyme and salvia, oregano and rosemary. She breathed in their scents with delight. How ingenious it was that the aromatic oils protected the herbs from the drought.

Her thoughts went to Setonius, who had taught her how to care for a garden. Euphrosyne had freed him as soon as she had arranged for her new house in Corinth, and he had done what he had dreamed of doing for many years, returning to his island and his gods in the Ionian Sea. He was away for a few months, then he came back to Euphrosyne, saying little.

He had told Mary Magdalene that everything there had been just as he remembered it, but that he had forgotten how limited it was. They had agreed that life offers no ways back.

He had then laid out a new garden in Corinth.

Mary felt a pain in her back, and as her mother had done, placed her clenched hand between her shoulder blades and stretched. As she did so, she heard horses clattering toward the street and a carriage screeching by her gateway. It was Livia, pale with scarlet patches on her cheeks.

'Mera is at the temple of Isis to give birth. But something's gone wrong. The child is lying wrongly and won't come out. She asked me to come and fetch you. Come quickly.'

Mary managed to wash her hands and face and pull a clean mantle over her shoulders before locking up the house and as usual giving the key to her neighbour.

'Leonidas knows,' said Livia as they set off. Mary could see she was shaking and took a firm hold of her sister-in-law's hand. She had nothing consoling to say and could only nod when Livia assured her the priestesses at the temple were known for their skill in the art of delivering babies.

Mary closed her eyes and prayed. To the almighty God of the Jews? She did not know.

The temple was a large circular building around an open courtyard, that was also circular. In front of the doorway to the delivery room was the bronze statue of Isis, alien and self-evident at the same time, glowing with inward-looking tenderness for the child in her arms.

They could hear Mera screaming with pain and fear. The two priestesses were trying to calm her, but their words did not reach her. One of them had her hand on Mera's belly, which was moving as if waves in a storm.

'Dear Lod Jesus, help me now.'

Mary did not know whether she had said it aloud, but that was of no importance. What was important was that he heard her.

'The pain will go now, Mera. But only for a moment and at that moment you must think about the birds sailing in the sky, about the trust they put in the winds. They are so sure that even the storm bears them as long as they can float in calm confidence with the wind. Now you are the bird and the force drawing through your body is the wind. Can you feel it, Mera, can you? Give way and go with it.'

Mera nodded.

'We must cut her,' said one of the priestesses.

'Do so,' said Mary, looking straight into Mera's eyes and using all her strength to keep Mera in the bed while the operation was being carried out.

'Breathe,' she said. 'Breathe calmly.'

It was over in a moment and the priestess nodded to Mary. 'The time has come to push.'

'The storm's coming soon,' said Mary to Mera. 'And you must go with it, not resist it. Now, can you feel the immense wind drawing through your body? It hurts, but is also magnificent. Go with it, help it, you're flying.'

Mera flung out her arms. 'I'm dying,' she cried.

Mary cried just as loudly into the girl's ear. 'No, I'm holding you. Go with it, keep pushing.'

The boy was born half an hour later, then bathed and shown to Isis in the doorway. As the child was carried out to the goddess, Mary felt a distance, a fear, but at the same time, she could sense his smile. He was laughing at her prejudices.

It was dark outside, the midnight hour, the child sleeping in his mother's arm. The last thing Mera said before she fell asleep was 'promise me you'll stay, Mary.'

'I promise.'

She was given a bed alongside Mera, soft bolsters and light covers. Before she fell asleep, she had time to think that God was born on earth with every child. She was awakened once during the night when the boy cried, hungry and full of life. But she had no need to intervene, and with almost reverence she watched Mera put the child to her breast, as if she had always known what to do.

Then they fell asleep, all three of them.

Mary woke at dawn with a sense she was being watched. Mera was feeding her son and gazing at Mary, her eyes glowing with joy. 'All that you taught me about the wind was fine.'

Then the priestesses returned with hot water smelling of essential oils and something else. What was it? Was it vinegar? Mary thought with surprise.

'We must clean up mother and child now. Meanwhile Mistress Mary can take a walk in the courtyard.'

It was good to go out into the fresh air and see the sun's rays spreading over the circular courtyard. In the middle was a big stone, black as ebony, and beside it an old woman kneeling, sunk in prayer.

I should be praying too, thought Mary. Giving thanks for help given. But she could not pray here at the heathens' sacred stone. At that moment, the old woman turned around and smiled at Mary. 'Your god surely has nothing against our goddess,' she said.

That was the first time Mary had begun to realize that the old woman could read her thoughts.

Then without knowing where it came from, she said: 'I once knew a man who said that in the beginning man created god and made him into his own image.'

The old woman smiled, almost laughing. 'Naturally, that's how it is. We create the gods we need and worship them as long as they fulfil our needs. That is what makes the Jewish God so magnificent. He is one, and he is all that man is, cruel and power-mad, good and full of mercy.'

Mary felt her knees giving way and she had to support herself on the stone idol. The old woman noticed and said: 'Come in with me and we shall have breakfast. It's a long time since you had anything to eat.'

Before they reached the doorway, the old woman stopped. 'It is dark inside,' she said. 'Let us stay here a moment and look at each other.'

Mary looked into the ancient face, the skin like dry leather, a broad mouth, and surprisingly good teeth. Her eyes were ageless and her gaze open.

The priestess looked at Mary, slight but stubborn and unbroken, despite her great loss. There was a certainty in those blue eyes, but also a strange impotence about her, like a ship washed into a harbour where no winds ever reached.

They went inside, the old priestess' room so dark it took some time for their eyes to get used to it. Circular walls here, too, dark as if in a womb. They sat in silence at the table as the food was put out. Mary was hungry. She took some bread, and as she bit into it, a foolish thought raced through her head. She would like to have the recipe.

Then she tried to give thanks for all the help her young relative had received, but the old woman did not want to hear. 'You have a strong god,' she said.

Mary had no time to think. For the first time since she had come to Antioch, the whole amazing story of Jesus of Nazareth swept through her as if from a spring that could no longer be stemmed. She did not weep, even when it came to the crucifixion. Not until she described how the disciples had rejected her and the other women did her voice break.

The old woman looked sad. 'I had hoped the new man of god would restore the womanly force on earth.'

Then Mary wept. 'Nothing will change,' she said finally. 'The apostles are Jews, rooted in ancient prejudices that woman has no soul and man is the only human being.'

'It's not just the Jews. The ancient goddess lost power all over our world. People free themselves from agriculture, from childbirth, and from the flow of life. We are heading for the time of the big city, for the era of the merchants.'

They were interrupted by a young priestess who told them the women from the harbour town had arrived and were waiting for the priestess in the courtyard.

The old woman explained. 'We bring the prostitutes here in groups and cure their diseases and injuries as best we can. They are given rest, baths, and new clothes. Unfortunately that is all we can do.'

Mary thought about Jesus' words and everything she had neglected. 'For I was hungry and you gave me meat; I was thirsty and you gave me drink. I was a stranger and you took me in. Naked, and you clothed me. I was sick and you visited me. I was in prison and you came unto me.'

As they parted out in the courtyard, the sun was already high. Another hot day had begun.

'May I come back?'

'Come early. The mornings are best.'

Mary crossed the courtyard, avoiding looking at the prostitutes and their gaudily-painted faces.

Livia, pale and tired, was sitting with Mera. The child was asleep. Mary said goodbye to Mera. 'I'll be back in the morning,' she whispered.

Leonidas was waiting outside in the street.

17

Mary did not take in the enormity of the morning's events until she told Leonidas about their talk. 'You told her!' He did not want to believe her. Mary sat in silence, then said with great certainty: 'She knew.'

Leonidas shook his head. 'I don't think the priestesses can see into the past,' he said. 'On the other hand, they're very clever at reading other people's minds.'

'That could be the same thing.'

'I suppose so.'

'I'm thinking of taking some of my ill-gotten money and giving it to their work with prostitutes in Seleucia.'

'You must do as you wish.'

His voice was curt as always when the talk came to the old tribune in Tiberias. She changed the subject.

'Are you pleased about the new child?'

'Oh, yes, for Mera's sake. And Livia's.'

She knew he found Mera's husband difficult, the boastful Nicomachus, who had a great many opinions and a lust for power, and whose influence in the merchant house would increase now that he had a son.

At dawn the next morning, Mary went through the portal of the Isis temple, and was at once taken to the old woman, who again offered her newly baked bread. That morning she had lit an oil lamp, but although it did not make much difference to those dark walls in the circular room, it did mean they could see each other.

'I've given your story much thought and would very much like to hear more about Jesus and his view of women.'

Mary thought hard, but could find no answer. 'He had no views on women,' she said in the end. 'He saw them as human beings. He never flattered them and was not protective toward them. He accepted people as he found them. He had no prejudices.'

The old woman laughed. 'He didn't have that manliness which constantly has to be defended?' she said.

Mary smiled and nodded. 'That's true. But he had great wrath within him.'

'Who was his mother?'

'She was a widow and a strong person. It's true of the Jews, too, that their women have invisible power.'

The priestess repeated what she had said the day before. 'It's not just the Jews. If women didn't have that power, then the injustices against them would be fewer.'

Mary laughed aloud. 'If women openly exercised their power, we would have war between the sexes.'

The old woman changed the subject. 'Christians talk about the kingdom of God that is soon to come?'

'Jesus talked about the new kingdom as if it were not of this world. The kingdom of heaven is near, he said. But that was misunderstood, like so much else. It was forgotten that he said that the kingdom of heaven is within us and the new kingdom among us.'

The priestess drew a deep breath and her voice was stiff as she said, 'It's important that you give your view of what happened.'

'I am writing it down. But it is becoming so personal.'

The old woman shook her head. 'Which means no one need take it seriously,' she said.

'There is one thing that makes the task difficult. I can hear him saying it – write no laws on this that I have revealed to you. Do not do as the lawmakers do.'

They parted and Mary went to see Mera and the child.

Livia had stayed with her daughter this second night after the birth of the child. She had decided to have a long sleep, out of relief about the child and that all had gone well.

But sleep evaded her.

Her anxiety over Mera and her husband kept her awake, that boastful cockerel, incapable of any awareness of anyone else. When he had been told about the birth of his son, he had invited all his colleagues in the house to wine and had gotten very drunk, then disappeared into the wild quarters of Seleucia.

Then there was Mary. Livia was honest enough to admit it was jealousy that drove her into dark thoughts of her sister-in-law. She had gone to Mera like a queen, prayed to some unknown god, and taken command. And all that talk about the wind had infuriated Livia. By no means do the winds carry the birds that have not learned the difficult art of flying, Livia thought.

Afterward, when the boy had been born, Mary had retreated into her usual humility. Livia detested the humble, suspecting that they were concealing an arrogant spirit.

In the end, however, she must have escaped her wicked thoughts. When Mera woke to feed her child, her mother was sleeping so soundly, not even the cheerful morning greetings of the priestesses woke her.

Mera felt great tenderness for her mother.

'She's tired. She's been very uneasy,' the youngest priestess said.

'Yes.'

Mera thought Livia would have good reason to be uneasy even in the future.

After their breakfast, Livia woke and managed to smile at her daughter and the little boy.

They were told that Mary had already arrived and was talking to the mother of the temple. Livia's eyes hardened. Two witches, she thought, of course they seek each other out. Then she was ashamed and tried to conceal that ugly thought behind a crooked smile.

Mera bathed her child herself that morning, lovingly and with sure hands. But that great joy she expected did not come to her. 'Mother, I won't go home with the child to the merchant house and Nicomachus.'

'But where will you go?' whispered Livia.

'You know he hits me.'

Livia drew a sharp breath, but they were interrupted by Mary knocking on the door and coming in with flowers, a vision of joy in herself. But she stopped halfway. 'Is anything wrong?' she said.

Livia collected herself, but her voice was unsteady as she said, 'The women of this family have a problem.'

Before she could say any more, the door was flung open and there was Nicomachus, drunken and noisy, stinking of stale wine and rage. The first person he set eyes on was Mary, and he went straight over to her.

'So there you are,' he shouted. 'Sanctimonious cow, you, who couldn't even give the family an heir. You needn't make any more efforts. Nor your bugger of a husband, either. There's an heir now, and that's my son.'

Four strong women soon removed Nicomachus and put him out onto the street.

'He'll find his way home, I suppose?' said one of the priestesses when they came back, and Mera replied that yes, he always found his way home.

A few hours later, Mera and her child were taken to Leonidas' house.

Mary said nothing about Nicomachus' attack on her, but meeting Leonidas in the merchant house, Livia was not so considerate, and she was frightened when she saw his reaction.

Only a few days later, Leonidas had a talk with Nicomachus, Mary was not told what was said at the meeting, only that Nicomachus was to move to the merchant house's office in Ostia to learn how the silk trade was run in that great harbour outside Rome.

'How did you get him to agree to it?'

'I gave him an ultimatum. He has been guilty of a number of irregularities here.'

Leonidas' tone of voice was curt and, as so many times before, Mary reckoned there was a side of Leonidas she had never known.

Mera and the child stayed with Mary for a few more weeks, so Mary found it difficult to concentrate on her writing. Not that Mera disturbed her. No, it was the child and his sweetness that kept her from her work. When he had the colic in the evenings and would not go to sleep, Mary walked him to and fro, singing and babbling to him. She had never mourned her own childlessness, but now that loss truly pained her.

There were other changes, too. Livia refused to allow Mera to live in a house as poorly guarded as Mary's, and with no servants to help in the house.

'I presume you think your innocence protects you from the evils of the world,' she said. 'But that hardly protects Mera and the child. Antioch is getting more and more dangerous every year, robberies and murders almost everyday occurrences.'

Leonidas backed her up, for he had long worried about Mary being alone in the unprotected house and about her walking

86

alone in town. So Mary had the guardhouse put in order and equipped it properly for servants.

Livia watched in surprise. 'You must be ashamed to have slaves,' she said.

'Yes,' was Mary's simple reply.

Terentius was a Nubian, tall and very strong. When Mary first greeted him, she reckoned she had never seen a more handsome man, bronze coloured, with the features of an Egyptian pharaoh. Then she realized whom he resembled, a relative of the statue of Isis in the courtyard of the Temple.

She liked him from the first moment, his wife, too, a fine-limbed graceful woman with modestly lowered eyelids.

What he and his wife thought of her she would never know. They were both mysteriously closed when it came to both emotions and thoughts.

She was soon able to admit it was good hearing Terentius' footsteps at night as he went around the house and garden. And it felt safe to have him a few steps behind her when she went to the synagogue and the marketplace. And she didn't have to do the cleaning.

Only the cooking she kept for herself.

Once, when she was putting dough into the oven and he walked past, she thought she saw a shadow of a smile on his face.

When Mera reluctantly gave in to her mother's demands that she should move back home with her child, Leonidas said, 'I want Terentius and his wife to stay here.'

Mary could hear from his tone of voice that he had been expecting protests, but before she could open her mouth he said he was not going to give in on that point. 'I've already told Livia that I want to buy them.'

When Leonidas had begun this conversation, Mary had been relieved, glad of the help and security the two servants gave her. It was when he said the word 'buy' that she said, 'May I make one condition?'

He said nothing, so she had to go on. 'I want us to free them. I think they'd stay and wouldn't demand higher wages.'

'If you're sure, then I've no objections.'

'We'll talk to them.

The conversation with the two Nubians did not turn out as Mary had expected.

They said they were pleased to be able to stay. They both liked being there and the work and the house. But they did not want to be freed.

When Terentius saw Mary's surprise, he told her they were used to belonging to a family, that it gave them security and protection. That was unusually many words to come from him, and Mary sensed it had cost him a great deal, both the words and the decision.

A time then came when Mary was to devote herself to writing, but already on the very first day she was interrupted.

Rabbi Amasya came to see her, alone, early in the morning, and as usual, he did not want to come in.

They sat in the garden facing the street, fully visible. He had a thick parchment scroll under his arm.

'We have had a letter from Peter, the Christian apostle. It's long and written in . . . somewhat incomprehensible Aramaic. Dialectal speech, I should think. I want to know whether you would undertake to translate it into Greek.'

Her first impulse was to say no. But then she heard the wind moving in the tall cypress trees and thought she could sense Jesus' smile. Then she remembered her talk with the old priestess and her own insight that what she had hitherto written was too personal, that her intention had been to try to give a portrait of Jesus and what he preached. So it might be important to compare that with Simon's.

So she nodded at the cypress trees and said to the rabbi, 'Of course, I'll try.'

She sat all day over the long letter. It was badly written, as Rabbi Amasya had said, and she snorted. Simon Peter was an uneducated man. Then she was ashamed, for Jesus would never have thought like that.

But another thought followed on her shame. It was the Master himself who had chosen the simple fisherman from Capernaum. What had Jesus seen in the man? His integrity? His strength? Yes. And something more, his great childish heart?

It took her a long time to read the letter. She stopped in surprise right at the beginning, where Peter confirmed that we were born again through Jesus Christ's resurrection from the dead.

And further on: 'You were not redeemed with corruptible things as silver and gold . . . but with the precious blood of Christ, as of a lamb without blemish, without spot.

'Christ also has once suffered for your sins, the just for the unjust, that he might bring us to God, being put to death . . .'

Mary had heard Leonidas say that Christians saw the death of Jesus as a sacrifice. But she had not realized the breadth of that teaching. For many years, she had brooded over why He had chosen that terrible death on the cross. The people of this new teaching did not have to brood. They had the answer.

But then she remembered that Passover in the great temple in Jerusalem, the house of God turned into a slaughterhouse, the animals bellowing, blood flowing.

Peter wrote a great deal on humility, but was that the same kind that Jesus had spoken of?

'Servants, be subject to your masters, with all fear; not only to the good and gentle, but also to the froward. For this is thankworthy for conscience toward God, endure grief, suffering wrongfully.'

'And you wives, be in subjection to your own husbands.'

Much of the long letter bore Jewish characteristics, a Jew who knew the Jewish laws speaking.

'. . . Ye are the chosen generation, a royal priesthood, an holy nation, a peculiar people; that you should show forth the praises of him who has called you out of darkness into his marvellous light.'

All afternoon, Mary worked on the translation, making great efforts to follow the Aramaic text exactly, finding the right meaning and the best words. But she was strangely agitated.

She slept badly that night. Leonidas was away in Rome and she had no one to talk to. The next day she checked what she had written, compared it with the original and sent Terentius with the manuscript and greetings to the rabbi. She had no desire to meet him or to discuss the matter.

But her unease would not leave her and she found it difficult to assemble her thoughts and go on with her own writing.

18

A week or two later, she was hard at work writing when she heard someone thumping on the entrance portal and a moment later Terentius came to report that the rabbi and two other gentlemen wanted to see her. The tall Nubian was looking solemn.

'Ask them to come in.'

In the first confusion, she could see only one of them, Simon Peter, who filled the room with his great body and forcefulness. Rabbi Amasya made an attempt to say they had come to thank her for the translation, but his words were drowned by Simon's voice.

'Mary, Mary Magdalene!' he cried.

He wept as he embraced her, falling to his knees and kissing her hands.

'My sister.'

Mary turned as white as a sheet and strangely rigid. She tried to say something that would lower the tension in the room, but her tongue would not obey her. Then when her eyes met Terentius, where he was still standing over by the door, she managed to whisper, 'We'll have wine and fruit in the pergola.'

She would never be able to recall the next moment, her head blank and her mind paralyzed. Simon Peter was still going on, kissing her hands and shouting to the world that at last they had found the disicple Jesus loved most of all.

The words penetrated her paralysis, and her anger made the blood throb in her veins. She flushed, sat down and stared at Peter, managing to keep her voice steady as she spoke.

'The last time we met,' she said. 'You called me a liar and sent me away.'

'Yes.'

Now it was his voice that was unsteady. 'Can you forgive me?' he whispered.

'I imagine we'll have to try to understand each other.'

The moment she said it, she realized that it was an invitation to cooperate with him. Did she want to? Did she have to?

Then Terentius arrived with refreshments. Mary served them with steady hands, and they all had a moment in which to deliberate.

Mary nodded toward the third man.

'I don't think we know each other, do we?' she said.

'My name is Paul.'

Mary drew in a sharp and audible breath. She remembered the rabbi and Leonidas talking about Paul of Tarsus, Christianity's great thinker, the man who was to lay the foundations of the new teaching.

'I have heard about you,' she said, managing to conceal her surprise. At first glance, Paul was an insignficant man, small, bowed, and with no special features. The large and dramatic Peter almost obliterated him.

'I have long wished to meet you,' said Paul. 'I want to hear your testimony on our Master.'

She could see his eyes were intelligent and penetrating, though she met them unswervingly as she replied.

'My images of what is incomprehensible are different and I fear they would offend you. I am far from as sure of anything as Simon Peter is.'

Simon interrupted. 'But you were the one he loved most.'

There was a long silence while Mary calmed her heart and collected her thoughts.

'Let us take what Simon says as an example of the way our opinions differ. As we in his retinue were ordinary people with small thoughts and much envy, there was a lot of talk about this, just whom he preferred, who was closest to him. Siblings squabbling,' she said, searching for words.

'When Jesus spoke of love, he didn't mean personal ties. He loved. His love couldn't be measured or directed. It included everyone, at every meeting. No more, or less, nor in any different ways from person to person.

'He was always totally present, at every moment, at every meeting. Whoever he met, however accidentally, was given his total attention and all his love.'

Paul smiled for the first time, and his smile transformed him. Mary went on. 'I have thought many a time over the past years that he was too great for us. We will never understand. We can only try to interpret. And we do that from the starting point of our own prejudices.'

She flushed suddenly, and Paul saw it was anger colouring her cheeks.

'When I translated your letter, it became so clear,' she said, turning to Simon. ' "You wives, be in subjection to your own husbands . . ." you wrote. Did you ever hear him say that? No!

He said . . . there shall not be woman or man here. He is the only man I have ever met who regarded women as human beings, with respect. He did not protect them. He never made fun of them . . .'

She turned to look at Paul again and went on. 'Think on it. He came to preach tolerance, humility, and love. And who exercises those virtues, if not the mothers?'

Paul's face had crumpled again, but Mary refused to be stopped.

'We were equal numbers of men and women disciples, and women constantly surrounded him. Right up until Golgotha, when most of his apostles deserted him. Around the cross we stood, his mother, Susanna, Salome, Mary, Clopa's wife, and me.'

'And John, you forget John.'

'That's true, John was there during the long torment. He was the youngest, the most childish, so understood most.'

There was a long silence. Paul was divided, but pulled himself together and finally spoke. 'Mary,' he said. 'May we come back? And may I bring my scribe with me? He's a young man, almost a boy. But he has quick fingers and I would like to have what you have to say in writing.'

'To put it together with the final account that is to be written?'

'Yes.'

'Then you are welcome.'

They decided on a time the next day and the men rose to their feet.

In the doorway, Paul asked one last question. 'I presume you had heard tell of Jesus when you sought him in Capernaum. Was that because you wished to be freed of your torments?'

'No,' she said with surprise. 'I was not in torment. But we had met once, and I was much taken by his singular being.'

'You had met?'

'Yes,' she said. 'In the Galilean mountains. By chance.'

Then she smiled. 'If there is such a thing as chance,' she added.

Mary had no one to talk to. Leonidas was not returning until the following week. She tried to eat the food Terentius brought, but was unable to. She was frightened.

I must be truthful. But I need not tell them everything.

She went to bed early but could not sleep. The memory was suddenly crystal clear to her, the shimmering images of their first meeting.

Part Two

19

It was the time after the great rains, the month in the spring when water leaped from hidden mountain springs and the land turned green. Mary had walked through the new grass growing in the meadows where thousands of sun-red anemones were in flower.

At the foot of the mountain, the ground was covered with golden crocuses. As she stopped to draw in their faint scent and harsh saffron, she could hear the streams racing down the mountain, and a little higher up the quiet murmur from the pools where the water rested before going on its way to the villages. The wells there would be filled and the people overjoyed.

She climbed a steep goat track that was so familiar, although she had never before seen any in these areas. Everything was familiar, the transparent air blue and quiet, the long lines of birds calling from the sky on their journey north, and the resident birds singing in the tops of the terebinths.

Setonius was following her like a shadow. He nodded, pleased when they came to the ledge by the pool. 'Here below the cliff, you can't be seen from the mountains. Nor from the road, where the high trees hide you.'

He was afraid of Jewish rebels. But Mary said calmly that it was many years since the warriors of Judas the Galilean had been active in the mountains.

'You needn't worry.'

'I'll be back in a few hours, and you have bread and cheese in your basket.'

Mary listened to his footsteps disappearing down the track and was glad of her solitude. She cupped her hands and slaked her thirst, took off her mantle and headcloth and lowered her whole head into the pool.

She washed her neck and arms and combed her fingers through her long flowing hair, then finally leaned back against the cliff wall to let the sun dry her.

Pink petals rained down on to her wet hair. She looked up and smiled at the young almond tree that had struck root in a crevice in the rock.

The tree was also familiar.

But there was pain in all this recognition. Her mother's voice – 'For lo, the winter is past, the rain is over and flowers appear on the earth; the time of the singing of birds is come and the voice of the turtle is heard in our land . . .'

They had ridden out of Tiberias early that morning, she and the gardener in their grey tunics and worn cloaks, over the backs of the donkeys great sacks of prickly twigs and dry branches. That had been Euphrosyne's idea.

'No sight is more common along the roads than an old man and an old woman collecting brushwood,' she had said.

She was right, as usual. No one had taken any notice of them, neither the Roman horsemen, nor the hurrying walkers on their important errands, nor the merchants in wagons drawn by donkeys on their way south to Alexandria or north to Damascus.

A good while before midday, they had found the turning and reached as far as Naomi's village. Mary had carried out her assignment and, unnoticed, had managed to hand over Euphrosyne's money bag to the poor peasant wife.

It had been at the meeting with Naomi that her mother's voice had caught up with her.

On the way home, Mary's donkey had injured a leg and begun to limp. Setonius had examined the creature but had been unable to do anything. That was when Mary had her idea.

'I'll stay here and wait in the mountains while you ride home and fetch another donkey.'

Setonius had been reluctant and said he could walk beside the injured donkey.

As Mary knew him so well, she had finally said that in spring she had always longed back to her childhood mountains and would really like to rest for a while by a stream.

She was now sitting there with her hands open to catch the petals raining down over her. She decided not to allow old memories to take shape, but would just remember with her eyes, ears, skin, and nose. Birdsong helped her, the water in the pool swirling around and splashing dew-fine moisture onto her face. For a long spell, she watched the quick lizards darting about on the cliff wall. She caught a scent, familiar and long forgotten.

Then she remembered that this was the smell of terebinths in the spring, and she thought it strange that she could have forgotten such an individual aroma.

She could hear the wild dogs barking up on the mountain, also a familiar sound.

Then, very slowly, she became aware that she was no longer alone. She turned her head and glanced over her shoulder. A man was standing there, smiling at her. She smiled back.

'I didn't frighten you?' he said.

She shook her head.

He spoke in Aramaic with a Galilean accent. He was Jewish, she could tell that, not only by the tufts on his cloak but also from the long curly hair and the gravity emanating from him. He was young, his smile like a child's. An innocent, she thought.

'I am Jesus of Nazareth,' he said. 'I have been to see my mother and am taking a shortcut across the mountain back to Capernaum.'

'Are you a fisherman?'

'You could perhaps say so,' he said, smiling again, a smile so light and swift she might have been mistaken if the light had not remained in the air between them.

'I am Mary from Magdala,' she said. 'But I live in Tiberias with my stepmother, and I have been carrying out an errand for her in a village near here.'

'You are a Jewess.'

It was a statement. She nodded and he went on. 'Your eyes are innocent.'

She pushed her fair hair off her face and met his eyes. 'The blue colour is deceptive,' she said. 'I have been a whore in a house of pleasure in the City of Sin. I was recently the Roman tribune's concubine. He died, so I was free and able to make an excursion into the mountains.'

Then she bit her tongue, her head whirling. Why did I say that? He will want to go now.

But he did not leave. He came closer and sat down on the rock beside her.

'Don't you understand? I am unclean,' she said, a sharper note in her voice.

He threw back his head and laughed. 'Your eyes don't deceive me. You're as innocent as a child.'

Surprised, Mary told him that was just what she had thought about him the first moment she had seen him, that he was like a child.

He laughed again, took a bowl out of his knapsack, filled it with water and drank. She looked over the brim of the bowl straight into his eyes, light, transparent. Grey?

Then he put the bowl down and, astonishingly, said, 'Why do people harbour so much guilt?'

'Probably because they are so wicked. And that in its turn is probably because they are nearly always afraid.'

He said nothing, as if waiting for her to go on.

In the end, he said, 'But you're not afraid?'

'That's perhaps because the worst has already happened to me.'

The silence was longer this time.

He did not take his eyes off her, and she thought she had never met such a serious person before. There was no way to twist words into simple truths with him. Every nuance was weighed up.

'I think people are most afraid of being rejected,' she said, her gaze unwavering. 'I have never belonged . . .'

'Not even as a child?'

'No. If you have yellow hair and blue eyes in a small Jewish village . . .'

She was suddenly miserable, an old, long-forgotten grief paining her and her voice gruff as she went on. 'I was unclean even as a five-year-old.'

He did not console her. She felt she had to tell him the whole story, but at that moment she was seized with a strange certainty. He already knows. He feels it all.

It was unreasonable, but she was quite sure.

She suddenly felt cold and pulling her mantle around her, she said, 'Tell me about yourself.'

'I haven't much to tell. But nor have I ever felt I belonged.'

'But you are Jewish!'

'Yes, I had the very best conditions. I was the eldest son and was born to take over my father's workshop. He was a carpenter, an ordinary man whom I never really knew. And yet he spent a lot of time on me. He taught me his skills, step by step. And I learned the scriptures from him. The Torah filled my ears. I know it all, but the beautiful words have never really fastened in my heart.'

'And your mother? What was she like?'

'She is strong. But there was always an unease in her eyes when she looked at me. She didn't like me being alone, that I didn't play like other children, but went about on my own.'

His smile was slightly melancholy as he went on.

'When Father died, I wasn't able to grieve as I should have done. Mother and my brothers and sisters reproached me, but I overcame that with no harm. Instead of doing my duty as the eldest son, I asked my brother to take over the workshop. I said goodbye to my family and started wandering south toward the deserts.'

'That was brave.'

'I didn't see it like that. I was obeying the voice of God, which had always spoken to me. I didn't realize it was God's voice selecting me out, or that others couldn't hear him – until the cold nights beneath the stars in the deserts of Judea. That was why they needed so many laws. I've just been back home, trying to get Mother to understand.'

'Did she?'

'She said she'd always known I was a strange child and that I had to go my own way. But she's worried about me, that I might go mad.'

Mary dared a question. 'How can you be so sure it's the voice of God you hear?'

'Because I know it so well.'

How childish he is, she thought.

'Yes,' he said. 'You've no idea how much is required of you to be like a child.'

'I probably have some idea,' she said, and she put her hand in his.

The simple touch raced through her body, and her desire lit up in her eyes. She took his head between her hands, held it quite still, and kissed his mouth. And what had to happen happened; her desire lit his.

'I have never been close to a woman,' he said.

'Come,' she said.

At first she had to help him, teach his hands to find her body.

102

But soon, gently and pliably, they were able to seek each other and find what they were seeking.

Afterward, he rolled over on to his back and laughed. 'I hadn't understood this.'

'That there is so much joy in your body?'

He closed his eyes and did not answer.

Mary stroked his face. She could see he was older than she had thought, and weary. He fell asleep, but Mary soon had to wake him.

'I'm sorry, but we can't sleep together here. My servant will soon be back to fetch me.'

Then she remembered the basket of fresh bread and soft cheese, and she said they were probably hungry.

They exchanged few words as they broke bread and drank of the fresh water from the stream. When they heard Setonius' donkeys clattering along the goat track up the mountain, he said, 'I can be found in Capernaum.'

She replied as she had to. 'I shall come.'

The next moment he had disappeared.

20

Mary did not get to bed in Antioch until the morning, and yet she was rested and full of light when she woke.

But when she was eating, her head cleared. She would have to watch her tongue when she met the apostles and their scribe.

It turned out to be easier than she had thought. Simon Peter began with a question: 'I was wondering about what you said when you met Jesus on your excursion to Galilee. Did your stepmother allow a young girl to wander in the mountains on her own?'

Mary could afford a broad smile. Now she knew where she had him.

'Of course not. I had a servant with me, our old gardener. And we were on donkeys. As we approached the steepest mountain we heard a stream and decided to ride on up for a while, rest by the water, wash off the dust and have something to eat. We had bread and cheese in a basket. While I was sitting there by the stream, he appeared, a young man walking from his parents' home in Nazareth to Capernaum. He sat down beside me and we started talking.'

Simon interrupted her. 'He drove the demons out of you.'

'Did Jesus say that?'

Paul noticed her flush of anger again. Simon's eyes wavered as he replied. 'I don't know. That was what was generally said among the disciples.'

Mary turned to Paul. 'You see how the myths already flourished even when he was alive. I was not possessed by any demons. I was happy because of the spring, the flowering fields.'

Then she went on.

'We talked about the ordinary things people talk about when they meet. Last night, I tried to remember what we said. It struck me that it was the only time I ever heard him talk about himself, about growing up in Nazareth, and his family.'

She noticed Paul signalling to his young scribe, and continued on.

'He said that even as a child he felt he was a stranger in the village. He had been different, a loner. His mother had worried about him and it wasn't until his father died and he left his family to wander in the deserts of Judea that he understood in what way he was different from others. The others never heard God speak.

'He said he had always pondered over why people needed so many laws and regulations. Now he had understood.

'You know how often he was critical of the scribes and the men of the law. The last time I met him, in a vision after his death, he said it again. "Write no laws on what I have revealed to you." '

Peter was uneasy now, and Paul raised objections. 'You can't build new teaching without any structure or system.'

'Maybe so,' said Mary, hesitating, but then continuing her line of thought. 'But we turn all reality into a system, even what is invisible. And as we are Jews, it becomes a Jewish system, based on laws and the hundreds of interpretations of them.'

'Write that down,' Paul said to Marcus.

Then Simon took over. 'Why did he leave his family?'

'He said he was obeying the voice of God.'

'What did he do in the desert of Judea?'

'I don't know. He was taciturn when he told me.'

'And you asked no questions?'

'I asked him how he could be so sure it was God speaking in him. He smiled and said he had always known it.'

'You told him about yourself?'

'I thought I would tell him about my father being crucified and my family killed by Roman soldiers. Then an incredible thing happened. I met his eyes and knew that he knew.'

She went on, herself amazed at the memory. 'At that moment I just accepted it, and never gave a thought to how strange it was.

'Then a little later, Setonius, my servant, interrupted our conversation by the stream. We had to return to Tiberias before darkness fell. When Jesus said farewell, he asked me to come and see him in Capernaum. Then we parted.'

'You didn't know who he was?'

'No. He said he was Jesus of Nazareth. And I had never heard of the new prophet.'

21

Mary stayed in the pergola as the evening wind blew in from the sea, cooling the house and garden. She was thinking how strange it was that it had not surprised her when she had realized Jesus knew her thoughts and all her memories.

Wherever he was, everything became natural.

She closed her eyes and could suddenly see it all in front of her, image after image, how they went back home, she and Setonius, Euphrosyne receiving them in the kitchen with pleasure and hot food. At table, Mary described her visit to Naomi, the child on her arm and another in her womb, and how full of fear she had been that some neighbouring woman would catch sight of Mary.

Euphrosyne sighed.

The entire household in Tiberias was decamping, some of the furniture already gone to Corinth, other pieces sold, packing cases stacked on top of each other in the big hall. In only a few months' time, they themselves would be on their way to the new house in Greece.

As they talked, Mary could feel her heart fluttering. How could she explain what had happened on the way home? And that she simply had to go to Capernaum?

'I need to talk to you.'

'We'll go to my bedroom as soon as we've eaten.'

There was nothing left in the room except the big bed. Euphrosyne sat down on it and Mary sat on the floor in front of her.

'Something strange has happened to me . . .'

She made an effort to be truthful and detailed. Euphrosyne listened and smiled.

'You met a man and fell in love,' she said. 'That's not as strange as you seem to think. And it'll pass. That you should marry a Jewish fisherman in Capernaum is unthinkable. Think for yourself, think what you told me just now about Naomi and her life in the village.'

Mary shook her head. She had not even considered marrying.

'He knew everything about me,' she said.

Euphrosyne smiled again and said that you could imagine things like that at the moment you fell in love. All that business of the flowers and the stream had probably added to the atmosphere.

She doesn't understand, Mary thought. She'll never understand. I must tell her as it is.

'Anyhow, I want to go to Capernaum and see him again.'

Euphrosyne rose to fetch an oil lamp and its light showed Mary her stepmother had aged, that she looked tired. And lonely.

I can't do this to her, Mary thought in despair. But I must.

'I suppose you can go to Capernaum then,' said Euphrosyne. 'A short trip.'

'Yes.'

'Did he have a name, this young fisherman?'

'He was called Jesus and was from Nazareth.'

Mary saw Euphrosyne's face at once turn white as she stood there by the lamp. She took a few uncertain steps toward the bed, flung herself down on it and called out to all the gods of Olympia – help us, help!

Mary had never before seen Euphrosyne lose her head, not even in the most critical moments over the past years. She was frightened.

'Go and fetch some wine, strong wine,' whispered Euphrosyne.

Mary raced down the stairs and found Octavianus in the kitchen.

'Euphrosyne wants some wine,' she said agitatedly.

Octavianus also grew anxious. In his world, his mistress was never upset. His hands trembled as he gave Mary the large jar of the best wine the house possessed.

By the time Mary got upstairs again, Euphrosyne had calmed down and was lying still with her eyes closed and her hands folded over her chest. Mary poured out wine and Euphrosyne took the goblet and emptied it in one draught.

'More,' she said. 'And some blankets. I'm cold.'

Mary tucked her in.

Euphrosyne took a few more gulps of wine, then sat up in the bed, propped up against the pillows. She was still pale, but her voice was now quite steady.

'Now Mary, you must listen carefully. These insane Jewish people have a great dream. The Messiah is to come, the man of god who is to free his people. Over the centuries, one saviour after another has maintained he is the one. But the Jews have always been disappointed.'

Mary nodded. She knew more about the Messianic dreams that Euphrosyne did.

'I'm sure,' Euphrosyne went on, 'you understand that this dream, or myth, or whatever you call it, attracts young madmen who take on the role and fill it with fair speeches, great promises, and new prophecies. I don't think they are impostors, not all of them. The most insane almost certainly believe they have been chosen.

'In a few years they are generally exposed and executed as rebels. That isn't unusual, believe you me.'

Mary nodded.

'I have a Jewish shoemaker,' Euphrosyne went on. 'As you know, at least some of the people in the Jewish quarter have become more friendly toward me since I ceased my activities. Well, old Sebastiol and I can actually talk to each other. I went to him a week ago to order new shoes for the journey. The old man had changed. It shone from him.'

She paused briefly.

'When I asked why he was so happy, he told me the Messiah had been born, in Nazareth of all places. His name was Jesus and he wandered between the villages talking so that people were amazed, making the blind see and the lame walk.

'Don't you see! Your Jesus is one of these mad barefoot prophets trudging around uneducated people saying he is a messenger of God. And like all the others, he'll face a cruel death.'

Euphrosyne at last fell asleep very late that night. Mary stayed beside her, strangely cool and clear-minded when she reminded herself what he had said, word for word. 'My mother is afraid I'll go mad.' 'I obey the voice of God. I have always heard it.'

At dawn, she wrote a letter to Euphrosyne. 'I'm going to Capernaum now, to see him through your eyes. Do not worry, I'll soon be back . . .'

When Euphrosyne read the note, she shook her head and when Setonius noticed her despair, she said, 'Mary's Jewish heritage has caught up with her.'

Mary could remember her long walk northward, every meeting and almost every step. She had dressed in worn grey clothes and had pulled her headcloth low over her forehead. Despite the early hour, there were a lot of people out and about, simple people who greeted each other. Shalom. Once an old man stopped, raised his hand and summoned God's blessing on her journey. They spoke in Galilean Aramaic and she answered in the same way. She had not forgotten the language of her childhood.

When the sun was at its highest, she took a rest by the lake and ate the bread she had brought with her. Her feet were not used to walking distances and they hurt her, her sandals chafing her heels, and the soles of her feet burning.

She sat on the shore with her feet in the water, thinking calmly and clearly about what Euphrosyne had told her. In her dreams of the day before, she had seen herself running straight

109

into the arms of Jesus, laughing and saying here I am. Now she decided to keep to the edge of the crowd of people surrounding him and listening without revealing herself.

That would not be difficult, for the old Jew in Tiberias had said people flocked in great numbers around him.

Nevertheless she was astonished when she got to the town on the northeast point of the lake. There must have been many hundreds around him, a wide circle of people with solemn faces, all their eyes turned toward the centre.

What surprised her most was the silence. It was so still you could hear the waves of the Gennesaret striking the stones on the shore.

As if they were all holding their breath.

She could not see what was happening. Cautiously, step by step, she started slipping ahead through the dense crowd. People were friendly and made way for her.

She finally caught sight of him. He was kneeling, his arms around a man who had collapsed in front of him. Rigid with terror, Mary watched, thinking it could not be true. But there was no mistaking it. The terrible pus-filled sores on the ravaged face and the bells around his wrists. He was a leper.

She was not close enough to hear what Jesus was saying, but could see only his lips moving as he put his face against the sick man's. Time passed, no, thought Mary, time stood still, but was anyhow lengthy, and in the end Jesus got up and pulled the sick man up with him.

It's not possible, Mary thought.

But she saw that the ravaged face was clean and the man's movements full of strength as he ripped off the despised bells. Jesus said a few more words to him and then turned around to speak to the women behind him. They nodded and went over to the man, and Mary realized that he was to be washed and given new clothes.

Jesus was swaying slightly as he stood there. He's tired,

thought Mary. He raised one arm in farewell to all the people and went up the road to one of the houses.

The crowd of people sprang into life, some calling out loudly to God, others praying in chorus, and here and there hymns of praise were being sung. Many people were weeping. As they finally dispersed into smaller groups to disappear in different directions along the mountains and the shore, their voices rose higher and higher in rejoicing, but not screams of excitement.

Mary wept, the tears making white streaks down her dirty face. After a while she found herself alone and clearly visible. But she found it hard to move, her body stiff and cold. Her legs trembling, she finally walked over to the women busy with the sick man.

'Can I help?'

An older woman smiled at her.

'My name's Salome. You're new here?'

'Yes. I'm Mary from Magdala and have walked here from Tiberias to see him.'

'You certainly look as if you needed help yourself.'

They were friendly to her, took her down to the shore, bade her sit on a stone and wash off the dust from her journey and cool her feet. After a while, one of them brought her bread and a beaker of wine. Mary did as Euphrosyne had done the evening before, emptied it in a single draught. Then she washed her face and arms and lowered her feet into the cold water.

It was pleasant, but she was incapable of thinking.

Or did not dare.

As dusk fell, Salome came back. 'We women have a tent on the slope up here. Come with me and you can sleep there tonight.'

Mary obeyed like a child.

She fell asleep the moment she had settled down on the sleeping mat in the tent, the low voices of women all around her like a lullaby. She woke sometime during the night but the calm breathing of the women all around her soon sent her back to sleep. When she finally opened her eyes, dawn had not yet come but the tent canvas was lighter and she realized morning would soon be there.

She was still unable to think, however much of an effort she made. She kept remembering Euphrosyne, her grief and everything she had said, but that served no purpose. She tried to remember her long walk the day before, but that had gone from her memory. Whenever she tried to concentrate on the miracle she had witnessed, the whole event turned away.

If he is mad, then I am also going mad.

Suddenly the light was yellow, the canvas of the tent a golden cupola above their heads and one after another the women woke. Mary had taken off her headcloth and they looked at her hair with wonder.

'It's like sunlight,' one of them said with delight. 'Are you a Jewess?'

'Yes,' said Mary firmly. 'I was born in Magdala just across the bay. My father was crucified during the rebellion and my mother and brothers were all killed by the Romans. I managed to escape.'

Her new friends cried out with dismay, poor child.

They did not ask any more and she was grateful to them for that. They all hurried to dress for morning prayers. Mary had difficulty putting her hair in order, so was late, but at last she was with the others out in the courtyard of a large house and in quiet calm prayer with them.

They were many, about twenty men and as many women.

But Mary had no time to count. Jesus arrived, stood in the centre of them all and started to pray, a simple prayer, in clear words asking God to bless the day and the work they had to carry out.

When he opened his eyes and looked around, he caught sight

of her. His smile was like the sunrise and he called out aloud: 'Mary Magdalene, you came!'

His joy was so evident, they all had to share it. He went straight to her, took both her hands in his and pulled her toward him.

'This is Mary, a woman I met and came to love.'

A surprised murmur ran through the disciples as he took her in his arms and kissed her.

Mary knew then that there was no longer any decision to be made.

22

When they had all again assembled in the pergola the next day, Paul firmly took the floor.

'I've thought a great deal about what you said about his love including everyone at every moment and on every occasion. But there are contradictions that are hard to comprehend in what he was preaching. When he received the message that his adherents had come to see him, he said – "Who is my mother? and who are my brethren?" He said to the man who wished to go and bury his father – "Let the dead bury the dead."

'And they say he said – "Think not that I have come to send peace on earth: I came not to send peace but a sword. For I have come to set a man at variance against his father, and a daughter against her mother, and the daughter-in-law against her mother-in-law. And a man's foes shall be they of his own household." Have you also heard him say this?'

'Yes.' Mary's voice was clear and unhesitating.

'How do you explain that?'

'I can only tell you how I see it.'

Paul nodded and Mary went on. 'I have previously told you of his wanderings in the desert. He said it was not until he first went there that he realized other people could not hear the voice of God in the way it constantly spoke to him.'

'That must have been frightening?' Paul sounded thoughtful. Mary nodded and went on.

'Yes. But it also provided him with important knowledge. He said he at last understood why people had made so many regulations and laws. Perhaps another insight also came to him. And he came to see that strong family ties entail a danger.'

She hesitated before going on.

'With us it is an almost total blending with our parents, and a tremendously stern demand for obedience. That in all layers in life, honouring your father and mother can lead to us remaining . . . immature.'

She went on hesitantly.

'But most of all, I think he turned against the way we reduce love to personal ties. He also said it is easy to love your nearest, but hard to love your nearest when you met him as a shabby beggar or a criminal.'

Paul looked doubtful, but suddenly Simon Peter spoke up.

'That was what he demanded of my brother and me. He said, "Follow me" and we did. We abandoned Father and his fishing boats . . . no one should think that was easy. Mother wept and Father raged. He needed us in his work, but we betrayed him and that was a shameful deed. Nearly everyone in Capernaum despised us.'

Mary gave Paul a warm look and said: 'It was the same for me. I had to write a letter to my stepmother to tell her I was not coming back. She had been good to me, a foundling she took care of as if I had been her own. And I knew she needed me. She was just moving back to Greece and I was to be her support in her loneliness and old age.'

Mary's eyes filled with tears, but pulling herself together, she went on. 'It's hard to explain what power Jesus had.'

'You think he meant that you have to defy your family to be free?'

'Yes. Be adult and independent. And that couldn't happen without strife or, as he put it: "A son shall be set against his father, a daughter against her mother . . ."'

Paul shook his head.

'It's true, what you say that he was both God and man. But I knew him only as a human being. As God he was as incomprehensible as God is. When we were wandering together, I didn't even try to understand. But afterward, over all these years, I have thought much about it.'

They fell silent. Paul was deep in thought when they suddenly heard the courtyard door slam and a voice calling: 'Mary, Mary.'

The three men saw Mary take off like a bird and almost fly down the steps. 'Leonidas, Leonidas.' The tall Greek took her in his arms and twirled her around, both of them laughing out aloud.

'I thought you weren't coming for another few days.'

'We had a good following wind north of Cyprus.'

Peter was disturbed. The two of them were indecent. He ought to have known he was in a heathen house. Paul's face also seemed to crumple more than usual. If he had imagined anything about Mary's husband, he had thought of a plump moneygrabber. But here was a Greek man of the world, superior, educated as heathens often are.

Only Rabbi Amasya was pleased and unsurprised.

Leonidas put his wife down and looked with surprise toward the pergola. 'Have we guests?'

'Yes, come and meet them.'

Leonidas greeted Rabbi Amasya with a warm embrace and then turned questioningly to the others. The rabbi introduced them, first Simon Peter, then Paul.

'Yes,' said Simon. 'You were one of those . . . foreigners who came and went, I remember.'

To Paul, the Greek said: 'I've read one of your letters and was impressed by your insight and clarity.'

Then he turned to Mary. 'We have distinguished guests and you haven't even offered them wine and fruit.'

'I'll do that,' said Mary, and hurried off, but at the door, she turned to the rabbi. 'You can explain,' she said.

While Amasya was speaking, Paul had plenty of time to study this Greek, a tall, gangling man, greying slightly but not bowed. His face was captivating, with its unusually heavy eyelids easily concealing his observant gaze. But his mouth would always betray him, finely drawn and ultrasensitive.

'I understood from Peter that you also knew Jesus? I'm very interested to know how he seemed to you?'

'He changed my life,' said Leonidas simply.

Then Terentius appeared with wine, fruit, and cakes. Mary served them and Leonidas mixed his wine with water before drinking it. 'The dust from travelling makes you thirsty,' he said apologetically.

The three Jews took a cake, drank wine, and departed. The Sabbath was approaching and they had much to do.

'I hope we may come back,' said Paul as they made their farewells.

'You're welcome the day after tomorrow.'

Mary arranged for a bath for her husband, who had gone out to the kitchen to greet the servants. He found a boy there with a large glass of milk and some bread.

'And who are you?'

'I am Marcus, Paul's scribe.'

The boy was scarlet with shame as he explained. 'There wasn't much to write today. And I was hungry.'

Leonidas laughed and said that hunger went with his age, and he was welcome.

Then he greeted Terentius and his wife. At that moment, Mary came into the kitchen and looked with surprise at Marcus.

'They've gone,' she said. 'They must have forgotten you! Why didn't you take any notes today?'

'I only write when Paul gives me a sign. And the moment you started speaking, he sent me away.'

'Did he now?' said Mary, looking thoughtful.

23

Leonidas went for his bath and Mary conferred with Terentius on dinner to welcome him home. They had fresh fish and a surplus of vegetables.

'You first,' said Mary at the dinner table.

Leonidas' mouth drooped and his reply was brief. 'A lot of business in Rome and great problems with Nicomachus. I'll tell you about it all later.'

His smile came back as he went on. 'In Ostia, I found a ship ready to depart to Corinth, just imagine. I got a cabin on board and a week later went to see Euphrosyne.'

Mary's eyes shone when he told her how pleased Euphrosyne had been and how happily she had settled in the lovely house and the new garden. She was well, strong and purposeful as always. She sent her warmest greetings to Mary and had sent a long letter.

'She's becoming Christian,' he said. 'Did you know?'

'Yes, I gathered that from her letters. I'd hoped we would be able to go there together before the autumn storms set in,' said Mary.

'We can do that. But you seem quite busy.'

'Let's take our wine and go and sit in the library. You shall hear everything that has happened from the very beginning.'

And that they did. Twilight fell, and it grew darker, but they lit no lamps. When Mary finally fell silent, he had clear pictures of what had happened. As usual, she had made notes of everything that had been said and had read them out to him.

'As you see, I haven't lied,' she said. 'Only left some things out.'

'Good.'

He lit the lamps. They looked at each other and smiled.

'I have to tell you there are great antagonisms between the Christians. Jerusalem's Jewish Christian congregation is the largest and the most powerful.'

That upset Mary, but he went on.

'Many of them think Jesus was the Messiah, God's messenger to the Jewish people. But Paul has another view. He wants the teachings of Jesus to go out to everyone. And the Christians are gaining adherents everywhere, here in Syria, in Cappadocia, in Sicily, yes, even in Rome. And in Greece. I heard about the conflicts from Euphrosyne's deacon in Corinth.'

'Do you mean that Jerusalem's Christians consider that everyone who converts to Christ has first to be a Jew?'

'Yes. They demand that Jesus' followers shall follow the laws, all the innumerable commandments on what is clean and what unclean. And they have to be circumcised, so as you can imagine, that is the biggest stumbling block.'

Mary listened, her eyes wide. 'I oughtn't to be surprised,' she said. 'Jerusalem's priests have always been strict. Where do his own apostles stand?'

'There's some hesitation there, too. But they say that Jesus urged them to go out into the world and make all the people his disciples.'

'Do you know what Peter thinks?'

'There's a story about Simon Peter and a Roman called Cornelius, an officer in the Italian cohort in Caesarea. One day an angel came to Cornelius and urged him to bring in a man called Simon Peter who lived with a tanner in Joppa.

'The next day, Simon Peter also had a dream. The sky opened and showed him a number of unclean animals. And a voice said: "Rise, Peter; kill and eat." Simon Peter refused: "I have never eaten any thing that is common or unclean." Then the voice said what God made clean, he, Peter, should not make unclean. You can see he pondered on what this vision meant. But no clarity came to him. A moment later, Cornelius' servant came to the tanner's house by the sea and gave him the Roman's message. Peter departed, went with him to Joppa and visited the heathen. When he heard about Cornelius' meeting with the angel, Peter said: "Of a truth I perceive that God is no respecter of persons, but in every nation he that feareth him and worketh righteousness, is accepted with him . . ." There were many people in the Roman's house and they were converted. Peter had them baptised and stayed for several days in Cornelius' unclean house.'

'That was good,' said Mary. 'Yet Peter still sees people through Jewish eyes.'

Leonidas went on. 'So, then there's Paul. He's at a disadvantage because he has never met the living Master. But he's the most intelligent of them all and is best at putting things into words.'

Leonidas fell silent for a moment, then winked at her.

'You must see that meeting you was a great event for him. They talk about you in the Christian congregations and like everyone else, he has heard that you were the disciple Jesus loved most. And he's sure to have been told that you went into open battle with Peter and left the apostles in Jerusalem. Then you unexpectedly appear here in Antioch. Here, suddenly, as a main witness who was not drawn into all those squabbles.'

Mary smiled. 'A woman. And married to a heathen.'

Leonidas laughed too, but said: 'Well, anyhow, your reputation is great. You'll do all right for his opinions.'

'I like him. And sometimes I find Peter difficult. He's so

dominating and so sure of himself. And yet, Leonidas, he has a light and a force . . . which I recognize.'

'So do I.'

Leonidas yawned and said they must go to bed.

'May I sleep with you?'

He was pleased, there was no mistaking it. She crept into his arms and he drew the covers over them. He fell asleep immediately. She lay awake, thinking that she had not told him what was perhaps most important to him. That her memories had returned, and she could see in clear images what had happened during her wanderings with Jesus.

24

As so often at this time, Mary woke long before dawn and went wandering with Jesus toward Jordan; it was hot summer in a bleak landscape, the dust flying and the road stony and hard on the feet. And yet it was easy walking.

After them came the disciples, all but Simon and Andrew. She remembered being surprised when she turned around and saw they were missing. Why? She could not remember.

They had to spend the midday hours resting in any shade they could find. But wherever they chose to rest, people assembled, appearing as if from nowhere, just standing there, the halt and the lame, the old bowed with their ailments, and the sick children with their sorrowing mothers. And as always, Jesus went from one to another, putting his hand on their heads and giving them health and new courage.

They reached the river and had to wait quite a while for the ferryman to come with his boat. Mary, sticky with dust and sweat, said, 'Let's swim.'

Jesus' followers shook their heads, but Mary had learned to swim in Tiberias. She looked expectantly at Jesus. 'Come,' she said.

He laughed and followed her down into the river. They swam, and despite the current it went as easily as a dance. Wet and cool, they reached the other shore, where the ground was soft with greenery and there were high cypress trees. They sat in the sun for a while to dry their clothes before seeking the shade under the trees.

They were seldom left alone.

The ferry soon arrived, seething with people on board, all of them wanting to see and hear Jesus. As so many times before, Mary thought – how does the rumour spread? How do they know? How do they always manage to catch up with us?

'With God's help,' Jesus said, and Mary nodded. But she could see he was weary.

He spoke in the synagogue in Bethsaida and Mary heard him say that man should not worry about the morrow: 'Consider the lilies of the field . . .' Mary thought that this was the core of his message, to have trust. And she remembered their first meeting and what she had experienced as she sat there alone by the stream. A state so self-evident and yet so difficult to capture.

They slept in an ordinary house on good bolsters. In the morning, Mary asked if they could return by boat across the lake, and Jesus nodded, admitting his exhaustion. It was a calm day with no wind. The disciples sat in silence in the boat slowly being rowed toward Capernaum, where more crowds of people were waiting. Simon was waiting on the shore and Mary swiftly got off the boat.

'Simon, can you disperse the people?' she said. 'Jesus must be allowed to rest.'

He nodded. 'Go in at the back,' he said.

Jesus slept for ten hours that night.

Why had she remembered that journey? It had not been

particularly long or strenuous, nothing compared with the long trail to get to Lydda on the coast or across Jericho to Jerusalem. Was it because for the first time she had worried about Jesus? He had complained and that was unlike him. 'The foxes have holes and the birds of the air have nests, but the Son of Man has nowhere to lay his head.'

But there was another reason why the journey to Bethsaida was so clear in her memory. When Jesus woke after his long sleep, he looked at her with a smile and said: 'Today a great joy awaits you. A man you love is on his way here.'

Mary thought for a long time, then shook her head. 'I have loved only one man before I met you. And he has been dead for many years,' she said.

Jesus did not reply, but his warm smile remained.

As they were having breakfast, Simon came to say that Capernaum had been visited by a whole group of scribes, sent by Herod Agrippa to spy, Simon reckoned.

Jesus laughed.

Some men were in the courtyard with a cripple on a stretcher. Jesus at once stopped, went over to the cripple and said that he should not worry, 'Son, your sins be forgiven you,' he said.

The learned men standing there waiting to greet the Galilean prophet screwed up their faces in horror, reckoning he was blaspheming.

But Jesus asked them why they bore evil thoughts in their hearts.

There was a long silence among all those who had assembled. But then they heard Jesus' voice. 'But that you may know that the Son of Man has power on earth to forgive sins . . .'

Then he turned to the cripple and said: 'Arise, take your bed and go into your house.'

The man rose and walked and the people praised God. Only the scribes remained silent, struck dumb, as if unable to believe their own eyes.

Afterward, Jesus walked along the shore and the people crowded around him. There were not only Galileans in Capernaum now, but also people from Judea, Idumea, and from the other side of Jordan; yes, people came to him all the way from Tyrus and Sidon. There were also heathens, Syrians and Greeks in the huge crowd.

Jesus was so hard-pressed that he got into a boat and spoke to them all from out on the lake, his voice never shrill, nor did he shout. No, his voice was light but could be heard at great distances everywhere.

At midday the crowds at last dispersed. Jesus was to go with his disciples up into the mountains. 'You stay here,' he said to Mary.

When he saw her disappointment, he laughed. 'Have you already forgotten what I told you this morning?' he said. 'Stay here, and wait.'

While Jesus and his disciples took a detour around the house, Mary went to her room to rest. At the doorway, she heard a voice she recognized, distantly, as if from a dream far back in childhood.

'Mary.'

In front of her was a tall Greek, but her eyes refused to take it in. Salome, standing alongside her, saw how pale she had become and put her arm around her.

'You have a bad habit of fainting the moment you see me,' said Leonidas.

It was the voice and the laugh that brought her back to reality, but she clung to Salome as she whispered to him, 'But you've been dead for eight years.'

'I wasn't killed, just taken prisoner. Can we sit down and talk together?'

Mary looked at Salome and quickly explained. 'This is my stepfather, Salome. He died in a war far away in the kingdom of Parthia and I have mourned him for years and years.'

'I see,' said Salome. 'I suggest you go down to the rock by the shore, where the two of you can be alone together.'

As she disappeared, they heard her calling out to the other women that Mary Magdalene's stepfather had come back to her.

Mary's knees were shaking and her steps down toward the Gennesaret were by no means steady.

'I am also shaken,' said Leonidas. 'I saw the cripple walking and I heard Jesus' words to the scribes and everything he said from the boat.'

'I'm so used to it, it no longer surprises me,' said Mary. 'Yet his words are the most amazing of all. No one has ever spoken like that before.' She fell silent, then said, 'No, what is most amazing is he himself, meeting him.'

Leonidas briefly described his capture by the Bedouins and the ransom his sister had paid to free him. Mary realized the explanation was plausible, but . . .

'It's a miracle, all the same, Leonidas,' she said.

'Yes.'

They were interrupted by Salome, who came with wine, water, bread, and cheese. Leonidas thanked her and they ate in silence. They soon heard Jesus and his disciples on their way back. Leonidas rose, drew his fingers through his hair and brushed the crumbs off his cloak. 'We must go and greet him.'

'No,' said Mary. 'He'll come here. I think he wants to see you alone.'

She was right. In a moment or so, he was there in front of them, laughing at Mary. 'Sceptic,' he said.

His astonished disciples up on the slope were able to see Jesus taking the tall heathen in his arms and kissing him on both cheeks. 'Your loyalty will receive its reward in the kingdom of heaven,' he said.

'There's nothing remarkable about this,' said Leonidas. 'I have loved this child ever since I first met her.'

Then he fell silent, confused now that he realized the other man already knew everything about him, observed every thought and knew everything he had been through.

Leonidas was filled with serenity and great happiness. He had never realized what a liberation it was to be totally seen through.

That same afternoon, Jesus and his disciples walked through the town. They happened to stop outside the customs house. 'As if by chance,' said Simon when he told Mary about it, but she already knew that nothing occurred simply by chance.

Outside the house was Levi the customs collector, also known as Matthew.

And Jesus said to the publican, 'Follow me.'

A while later, Levi invited the Master and his disciples to table in his house, and many customs collectors and other sinners were there together with Jesus. Naturally, this caused a great stir.

From the very first, Mary took a liking to Levi, a small man, a great mildness in him, his face bony but his eyes full of warmth and wisdom. She at once felt that the affection was mutual. Both of them, two sinners.

Leonidas had retreated into the crowd of followers, but he stayed fairly near the front when Jesus was speaking that evening on the hillside above Capernaum.

'I thank thee O Father, Lord of heaven and earth,' he prayed. 'For thou has hid these things from the wise and prudent, and hast revealed them unto babes.'

It was challenging. Leonidas glanced at the scribes who had gathered in a large group quite close to Jesus, but their faces were closed, and if they showed any emotion, it was surprise.

They were simple words, easy to comprehend. 'Come unto me, all you that labour and are heavy laden, and I will give you rest. Take my yoke upon you and learn of me . . .'

But there were also sentences that went beyond Leonidas' understanding.

'Neither do men put new wine in old bottles, else the bottles break and the wine runneth out . . . but they put new wine in new bottles and both are preserved.'

Leonidas found sleep difficult that night, not because he was in a tent with other men, for he was used to that, but because the day's events kept him awake.

The next day came with yet another overwhelming event. With his own eyes, he saw Jesus bring a little dead girl back to life.

He had only a few brief moments to talk to Mary. He was full of questions and she stroked his face to console him. 'Don't ask,' she said. 'There are no answers that we can find words for.'

'Just one thing, Mary. What did Jesus mean when he said that the reward for my loyalty will be great in heaven.'

'He usually says that the kingdom of heaven is within us.'

By the time Leonidas had departed to return to Antioch ten days later, he was a new man, with no bitterness, feeling strangely empty of protests.

'I'll be back.'

Mary smiled.

'Of course you'll be back,' said Jesus.

Leonidas rode to Caesarea and found a ship on its way to Seleucia. Again, he found it hard to sleep that night. He stood on deck, looking over the sea and up at the stars. There, suddenly, he realized what Jesus had meant with his talk of new wine that must be poured into new bottles.

25

Far earlier than had been agreed, at the fourth hour on Sunday, Paul was knocking on Mary's gate. He apologized for disturbing her so early and said he had come to postpone the afternoon's meeting. One of his closest collaborators had just arrived from

Cyprus, a man called Barnabas, a clear thinker and a man of action.

'He's going to help us organize the Christian congregation in Antioch. At the moment, he's reading the notes Marcus made of our talks with you.'

'Are there many here being baptized?'

'Yes, Antioch already has the largest congregation outside Jerusalem,' said Paul with one of his rare smiles.

Then he said he wanted to take up the question that had been worrying him since their previous meeting. 'It's rather personal,' he said.

She was surprised, but did not show it. She asked him to go and sit in the pergola and went to fetch cool drinks.

It was a hot day.

'I had a difficult and antagonistic relationship with my father,' he said. 'Now you say that Jesus encouraged us to oppose our parents.'

'Not oppose, but make ourselves free.'

'Isn't that the same thing?' Mary could hear the bitterness in his voice.

'I don't know,' she said finally, 'whether freedom has to entail a break and all the misery which that brings with it. But I'm probably not the right person to understand how difficult it can be.'

She gazed into the distance, as if trying to capture evasive memories.

'I yearned for my mother,' she said. 'But she was dead. So I directed my longing into a dream in which she was strong and perfect. Nothing bad could have happened to me if she had been allowed to live.'

She smiled before going on.

'A long time went by before I understood that nearly everyone had the same dream. People with living parents also had childish fantasies about their father or mother being omnipotent. Like

God himself. Sometimes, when Jesus talked about us having to be free to be able to grow, I've thought perhaps it has been useful for me not to have any parents.'

Paul looked frightened. 'But those who break free have to pay a high price,' he said.

'Guilt?'

'Yes.'

'I think Jesus meant that instead of being paralyzed by guilt, we could reconcile ourselves to it. Forgive ourselves and thus our fellow human beings.'

She was suddenly eager. 'You know the blessings in the Sermon on the Mount. "Blessed are the poor in spirit, for theirs is the kingdom of heaven." I understood that to mean that people who could see their own guilt could open themselves to the kingdom of heaven.'

She looked straight into Paul's eyes and saw they were full of doubt.

'I need time to think about what you've said,' he said and he took his leave. They would meet again the next day to talk, and he would bring Barnabas with him.

Mary went with him to the gate, and before they parted, he said: 'What you're saying is hard to understand. We can't take such teaching out to the people.'

Mary smiled. 'Even I realize that,' she said.

She watched the bowed figure disappearing down the street, and just as she had thought the first time they had met, she reckoned he must be suffering from some painful illness.

She made a detour through the garden before going into the house, and on the top terrace saw Terentius going around with a big watering can.

That was good. She tried waving a thank-you to him, but he pretended not to notice. She sighed, thinking as she had so often that she would never learn how to behave toward servants.

She finally went into her writing room to make notes on her

conversation with Paul. But once there in the shady room, she just sat there with her images of the day when she had first met Jesus' mother.

26

Dawn in Capernaum, light mists rising from the lake and enveloping houses and harbour in a gentle grey light, and despite the early hour, people were already gathering in the courtyard.

Jesus was still asleep. Mary slipped quietly down to the kitchen to prepare his breakfast. She could hear the expectant murmur from the crowd already assembled in the courtyard. They would soon be calling out for him, but she had learned now to refuse them, even refuse the Master.

When she took the food up, he was already up and washing.

'It's going to be a long day,' he said.

'Yes. And you're not to go out until you've eaten – two eggs, bread, and cheese.'

He smiled at her. 'May I not have anything to drink?'

'Oh yes. Salome has made some apricot juice.'

But he did not eat at all, his appetite poor at the time, but she coaxed him and he obediently drank the juice.

She heard him talking to the people while she was washing his clothes by the well. She found a tear in his mantle and was about to find Susanna, the best of them all with the needle, when she heard voices calling – 'Behold, your mother and brethren stand without, desiring to speak with you.'

And then she heard him answer: 'Who is my mother and who are my brethren. . . ? For whosoever shall do the will of God, the same is my brother and my sister and my mother.'

Mary Magdalene's blood froze. Those were terrible words.

But she went over to the women, the torn mantle over her shoulder, to look for Susanna. The women had also heard those fearful words and were sitting as if paralyzed. Mary, Clopa's wife, went to find Mary of Nazareth, for they were related, and they all knew what Jesus' mother would be feeling. Mary Magdalene showed Susanna the tear and Susanna took the mantle, relieved to have something to do.

Clopa's wife, Mary, finally found Mary of Nazareth on the edge of the crowd. She was difficult to persuade, for she had already decided to go back home.

'But you must be tired and hungry after walking all the way across the mountains last night. Come with me and you can rest. And eat.'

She allowed herself to be persuaded and went with the women to the shore to wash her feet and face, and brush her greying brown hair, largely out of habit, for she was not a woman to take an interest in her appearance. Yet she was beautiful, not as was so often said of older women that traces of a vanished beauty could be seen, but no, she was more beautiful now than ever, thought Mary Magdalene.

Mary of Nazareth gazed from woman to woman, as if seeking someone. Then her eyes fell on Mary Magdalene, who was thinking how alike mother and son were, the same grey transparent eyes and the same upright stature. 'Are you the whore my son lives with?'

'Yes, but I'm no whore.'

Despite her exhaustion, Mary of Nazareth could sense the resentment of the women now gathered around Mary Magdalene. 'I would like to talk to you in private,' she said.

'We have a room upstairs in the house. You're welcome to come there after you've eaten.'

Mary Magdalene's heart was beating fast, but she walked calmly to the well to hang the washing out to dry, then just as calmly she went up to the room, put away the dishes and rolled up her sleeping mat. On a sudden impulse, she took off her headcloth and combed out her challenging fair hair. When she heard the other woman's footsteps on the stairs, she remembered Jesus' words: 'Love thine enemies; turn the other cheek.'

Now I have to see whether what he has preached has had any effect on me.

She was angry, full of scarlet rage.

She placed the cushions on the floor and asked the other woman to be seated. They sat down opposite each other and Mary Magdalene's gaze did not waver from the other woman's face.

'I know a little about you. You were the concubine of the Roman tribune in Tiberias before you met my son and seduced him. Do you deny it?'

Mary Magdalene was suddenly quite calm, almost cold, choosing her words carefully before answering.

'The tribune was over eighty and half-paralyzed. He had heard that I spoke classical Latin, so every day I sat at his bedside reading the poems from the *Aeneid*. I bathed his forehead and changed his pillows. I held his hand when his pains were severe. The malicious rumours began to fly across town, to the despair of my stepmother.'

Mary of Nazareth had a scornful reply on her tongue, but swallowed it. Something in the girl's gaze told her she was telling the truth. Yet she had to say, 'But you helped a heathen and an enemy.'

'I gave comfort to an old person for whom life was difficult.'

'You mean you did it out of pity?' Her voice was scornful, but Mary Magdalene went on just as calmly.

'It wasn't that simple. You must know that almost no one in this country dares say no to a Roman officer. I was afraid at first, but after a while I just felt . . . compassion.'

Silence fell, then Mary Magdalene spoke again. 'When you say I seduced your son, I have to assume you don't know him well.

Jesus does not allow himself to be seduced, persuaded, or deceived by anyone.'

Mary of Nazareth hid her face in the corner of her cloak and Mary Magdalene saw she was crying. 'You're right,' Mary of Nazareth went on. 'I've never known him, not even when he was a child. It's a frightening feeling, always, not being able to understand your own child.'

Mary Magdalene said nothing and let time pass. Then the other woman unexpectedly spoke again.

'Do you understand him?'

'No, no one can. He is too great for us. And I accept that.'

'It's hard for a mother to think like that.'

'I realize that.'

'Children are a part of their mother, her body, her dreams and . . . her mind. I had given birth to a stranger.'

Mary Magdalene leaned forward and took the other woman's hands in hers, then said in a voice that was unexpectedly solemn, 'You were born to a great task, Mary of Nazareth. You must have been chosen.'

Mary's face changed, her gaze going long back in time. She's remembering, thought Mary Magdalene. But Mary's eyes closed. She was not going to tell her story. All she said was, 'I was fifteen.'

Then they heard that Jesus had fallen silent out in the courtyard and Mary Magdalene said, 'Come, come with me and you can see what he does for the sick and the wretched.'

They were both quite close to Jesus as he made a blind man see, a lame man walk, and cured a woman with a skin disease. Mary of Nazareth saw it all happen, her face white and lips pressed close together. As if holding back a scream, thought Mary Magdalene.

The day grew hotter and it was approaching the sixth hour when the crowd dispersed and out of the crowd appeared both his brothers, weighed down with wonder.

But Jesus went first to greet his mother. 'I see you have become friends,' he said to the two women.

'We have come to understand one another,' his mother said. 'And I have learned a great deal.'

They had a light meal together, the mother, her sons, and Mary Magdalene. Little was said at table, as if they were all absorbed in their own thoughts on what had happened that morning. Finally Mary broke the silence, rose and said: 'The sun is already high in the sky. It is time we all went to take a midday rest.'

The mother turned to look at her eldest son and saw what Mary Magdalene had seen. He was very tired.

In the afternoon, they had another talk, this time with Mary, Clopa's wife, Salome, and Johanna, the wife of Cusa the administrator.

Mary of Nazareth told them that the rumours about Jesus had become more and more malicious in the town. One day the old rabbi had come to see her in the village, and they had sat in the workshop, her sons interrupting their work to come and listen.

They were told that the Sanhedrin, the Jewish council in Jerusalem, had sent learned men to Galilee to test Jesus.

The rabbi had said that this had happened on the orders of Herod Agrippa himself, the king responsible for exposing every suspect rebellion against the Romans.

Clopa's wife cried out aloud. 'But a child could see that Jesus is no rebel.'

'As you know, the king has had John the Baptist executed. Rumour has it that he and my son together baptized the rebels in Jordan. And that some of John's disciples have now joined Jesus in Galilee.'

The woman sighed. It was true. They found John the Baptist's disciples difficult, hard men with burning eyes. It was also true that more and more learned men were joining them and often came into dispute with Jesus.

'Did your rabbi know the envoys had to report back to Agrippa and the priests of Jerusalem?' It was Mary Magdalene whispering.

Mary of Nazareth closed her eyes tight, as if trying to hide the fear in them.

'Yes,' she said. 'They say my son is mad, possessed by demons. That he carries out his miracles with forces from Beelzebub. That he sets son against father, daughter against mother. That he breaks the laws, does not keep the Sabbath, and constantly talks about the new kingdom that is to come. His list of sins seems endless.'

'What do you yourself think?' said Salome.

'I don't know. I have always feared for his sanity. But then I have seen that what he does is good. When I left home, it was to warn him. Today I have realized that I do not reach him, that I never have. My hope rests in Mary Magdalene.'

Mary Magdalene nodded, but said nothing about Jesus already knowing, that there was no one whose thoughts and opinions he did not know. He was going with open eyes straight into the fate that was his.

Salome came to her aid. 'No one can influence him.'

'Nevertheless I can try.'

Then Jesus returned. He had been wandering in the mountains with some of his disciples. The women went to prepare the evening meal and Mary Magdalene went to meet Jesus, who took her in his arms and kissed her.

'Have you some time for me?'

They were unusual words coming from her, and he smiled in surprise, saying he always had time for her. Together they went to their room and she told him what his mother had said.

As she had expected, he was not surprised, but when he saw the fear in her eyes, he asked her: 'What do you think I should do? I must obey God.'

They sat, saying nothing for a long while; then he said, 'I, too, am afraid, Mary.'

27

Mary immediately liked Barnabas. There was a mocking glint in his eyes that reminded her of Leonidas.

He has a sense of humour, she thought.

Tall and gangling he was, too, his face handsome and very Jewish, a finely-curved nose and warm brown eyes.

He said he was a Levite, born and raised in Cyprus, and his real name was Joseph.

'So you became a consoler and were given the name Barnabas,' she said.

His eyes glinted when he replied that Barnabas also meant exhorter.

Mary laughed.

'Go on, go ahead and start exhorting,' she said. 'You've read Marcus' notes about what I've said, and I presume you have some objections.'

He said what Paul had said. 'Your interpretations of the teachings of Jesus are interesting, but difficult to understand. People need simple rules and promises they can understand.'

'New laws, you mean?'

Mary flushed as always when she was upset, and her voice rose as she went on, emphasizing every word. ' "Woe unto you, also you lawyers, for you lade men with burdens grievous to be borne. Woe unto you, lawyers, for you have taken away the key of knowledge: you entered not in yourselves, and them that were entering in you hindered." '

Barnabas also went red in the face. 'What in the name of heaven are you saying now?' he cried.

'I'm quoting word for word what Jesus said to the scribes. Simon, you were there. You can't have forgotten!'

'I don't remember as well as you do. But that was largely what he said. I remember because I was frightened.'

'I can quite understand that,' said Paul.

Barnabas, the preacher, sighed deeply. Only Rabbi Amasya looked pleased. 'I can quite imagine becoming Christian just because of those words,' he said.

There was a long silence before Mary said in a calmer voice: 'I also understand the new teaching has to have stability and structure. But it mustn't become one of those religions whose task it is to keep people in order. I presume you've kept records of all his parables, as Simon Peter and the others remember them?'

They nodded.

'In my opinion, they all amount to one and the same thing, that people are self-sufficient and have a responsibility. And that there are no guarantees of reaching God by following all the rules and laws. That it can be the other way around. Think of the prodigal son, of the servants who were paid equally although some worked for an hour or two while others worked all day.'

Barnabas leaned over toward her. 'Do you think,' he said eagerly, 'that you could write down his parables as you remember them?'

'I'll try.'

They mixed their wine with water and drank. It was hot despite the shade in the pergola.

Then Paul spoke. 'In your opinion, what was most important in his teaching?'

'Reconciliation and forgiveness, what we talked about yesterday. You have to start with yourself, admit your fear and your selfishness. Regret what has happened and forgive yourself. When you can do that, you have no need to blame others.'

'You've talked about this before and I think you're right,' said

Paul. 'But it's difficult, almost impossible. How can we ever be reconciled with the evil we have committed?'

'With God's help,' said Barnabas.

'Yes. And by believing in yourself, in the kingdom of heaven within you,' said Mary.

Simon Peter shook his head. 'The kingdom of heaven is within you. He often said that, but I never understood it.'

Mary leaned eagerly over toward him. 'Do you remember that time when one of you, I think it was Andrew, asked Jesus where the new kingdom was and when would it come. And he answered that it was already there among us. That was true, Simon. I've thought so much about it, about the love that was there among all of us who followed him.'

Then Leonidas appeared back from the merchant house and interrupted their conversation. 'Am I disturbing you?'

'No, not at all,' said Paul. 'On the contrary, perhaps you can help us sort out the concepts.'

Leonidas greeted Barnabas, who rapidly repeated what they had been talking about. 'I presume you know what Mary thinks. But a church can't be built without definite rules and sure messages.'

Leonidas shook his head. 'It's difficult,' he said. 'I followed Jesus for various periods, and I listened with my whole being to everything he said. It was astounding. It turned my world upside down. On my journeys back to Antioch, I tried to bring him down to earth. I remember thinking it was his authority that obscured my clear Greek thinking.'

Leonidas laughed. 'Naturally I didn't succeed,' he said. 'His words grew in me, like the mustard tree he spoke of. It was a process. I don't think you can acquire his teaching through instruction.'

'So what do we do?' said Barnabas, the glint in his eyes becoming an ironic smile.

'Do as you have to,' said Leonidas, smiling too.

He thought for a moment before going on. 'You have an almost impossible task. The trouble is we human beings can't think unless we have a model, a pattern. We glide mercilessly into old ideas and then feel relieved because we think we've understood.'

'Do you think you can think in new ways as well as the old way?' said Barnabas.

'Jesus did. He made the world new and so he was a subverter of society. I can understand the priesthood in Jerusalem and their horror. Jesus is dangerous to the Jewish community. The balance between the Sanhedrin and the Romans is fragile and they could not risk it.'

The Jewish men around the table in the pergola held their breath, but Leonidas went on untiringly. 'Then we have the spirit of the day, and there we all have a weighty inheritance. You Jews with all your laws, we Greeks with our naive faith in logic and reason. And last but not least, the Romans who live in their blind faith in Roman order and discipline.'

He sat pensively for a moment before going on. 'In this world of rules, reason, and discipline, people's longing for miracles increases. It's quite natural that more and more people seek out the mystical religions of the East.'

They sat in silence until Leonidas finally threw out his hands in a gesture of abandon. 'Sometimes I've thought Jesus came too early into the world, that the world is nowhere near mature enough to understand him. The gods we worship are distant, cool. But Jesus' god is concealed in every heart. He exists in life, almost never admitted.'

That rare smile of Paul's appeared. 'Now you've forgotten what you yourself said about the mustard tree.'

As usual, Mary went with her guests through the garden out to the gate. Paul stopped for a moment under the great fig tree. 'Those words he said about his mother and brothers,' he said to

Mary. 'They must have hurt you, too, you who were his . . . chosen person.'

'Yes, it hurt, for a long time. Not until the rains came did I understand and accept that he couldn't have any chosen person.'

Mary slept soundly that night, the longed-for cool come at last to Antioch. But, as usual, she woke before dawn and once again went back to her memories.

28

Autumn descended on Capernaum and the winter rains were soon washing over the houses and lashing up the waters of the Gennesaret.

Leonidas was home and had long talks with Mary, as well as with Simon Peter, who was uneasy about the threats to the Master, the obscure words he had spoken on his suffering, though also about his exhaustion.

Leonidas had a friend who owned a house by the river not far from Bethsaida, a Syrian still serving in the Roman cohort in Caesarea. Leonidas sent a message to him and was given permission to borrow the house.

So it came about that the two of them had some time to themselves.

They slept a lot and laughed a great deal in the Roman bed in which the ample bolsters made it difficult for them to find each other.

She told Jesus about her dreams.

'I often dream about the sea,' she said. 'I go down to the shore and look over the great expanse of water and feel cleansed.'

'It's the same in the desert,' he said. 'Human beings become natural there, too.'

He smiled at her, and she knew he enjoyed the silence of this isolated house.

It rained, the water drifting in gusts across the garden and house and clattering on the roof. Sometimes it stopped and a pale sun glittered in the drenched garden. Jesus sat in the doorway, watching the thirsty soil drinking and the rainbow arching across the sky.

But then one night Mary was devastated by her first nightmare. She saw him abandoned, mistreated, and humiliated, nailed to the trunk of a tall tree. She woke in a cold sweat and in unbearable anguish.

He was asleep, thank heavens.

But the next night her screams in her sleep woke him and he took her in his arms. 'Tell me what you saw,' he said.

'Darkness, a strange darkness over a large town. It's an earthquake. You. You have at last been allowed to die, freed from your tormentors and the torture.'

Slowly, he roused her into the ordinary daylight of the peaceful house.

Weeping, she told him her dreams, the humiliations, his insufferable pain, and her own despair.

He has to console me, she thought. He must say that dreams are of no importance.

But he said, 'Your dreams know more than you do.'

She turned silent and very cold. He wrapped a blanket around her shoulders and put his arms around her, then a little later said: 'It's difficult for me to understand. Why do people live outside their own nature?'

She could only just manage a whisper. 'How could we do anything else?'

At their morning meal a while later, he talked of his mother. Her power over him and his mind had been the greatest temptation. How easy, so easy it would have been to be a good son, become a carpenter as the intention had been, and to please her, free her from her anxiety.

'The power mothers have over their children is great,' he said.

They sat in silence, listening to the patter of the rain on the roof as it gradually slowed to a few individual drops, and the winds rustled through the wet treetops.

He opened a shutter and smiled at the sun. 'Come and look, Mary.'

They walked hand in hand through the garden and for a few short moments she could be present, like him. But only in glimpses, then the hideous anxiety over the future took over.

After she had cleared and washed the dishes, she realized why he had spoken about his mother as a great temptation. It was not only the devouring mother threatening him – it was her, too, the woman who loved him.

The next night she was able to sleep without nightmares. When she told him in the morning, he smiled and said the dreams were no longer necessary, the message had been received.

She dared to ask. 'What did you mean when you said that people lived outside their own nature?'

'But you know that. Man's real nature, the innermost core, is of God. From there speaks what I call the voice of God.'

'To everyone?'

'Yes. But they have isolated themselves, and don't listen.'

'They daren't,' said Mary. 'Their security lies in the conviction that they can control life.'

'I've realized that.'

Then, almost despairingly, he said, 'Mary, I had no inkling man was so evil.'

The heat increased each day, the land greening and the first anemones opening their red perianths in the new grass. The time had come to leave.

The disciples gathered around him.

They headed toward Tyrus, he perhaps influenced by her longing for the sea. A man was sowing corn in a field and Jesus looked at Mary.

'Verily,' he said. 'Verily I say unto you, except a corn of wheat fall into the ground and die, it abideth alone: but if it die, it bringeth forth much fruit.'

She understood, but his words were no comfort to her. He noticed. 'My soul is also full of unease,' he said.

Then after a long silence: 'You must all take up your cross and follow me.'

At that moment, Mary realized why her dream had shown him nailed to a tree. He had chosen the worst of all deaths, crucifixion.

Levi looked at Mary. 'You're pale and tired,' he said. 'Let us take a rest.'

They found a stream on the hillside. The always compassionate Salome gave Mary a drink and massaged her arms. She was cold, as white as a sheet and Jesus looked at her with eyes dark with sorrow.

The rumour that Jesus was again out on his wanderings had spread and everywhere people gathered around them. Once again the unhappy, the sick and the despairing crowded around the Master and as usual, he went straight out among the tormented, relieved them of their guilt and cured their illnesses. Mary watched his acts of faith healing as if seeing them for the first time.

His immense presence is what achieves the miracles, she thought. He meets them all individually, sees their suffering, senses their question: 'Why does life treat me so badly?' The moment he gives his hand to the sick, they are in total fellowship.

Presence is perhaps the innermost form of love.

As the crowds grew, Jesus spoke. His words go right into the listeners, to their very nature, Mary thought, and she at last understood why he always told stories. God's speech cannot be shut into formulations, for it has various meanings and has to go along the road of images. Jesus painted, sometimes amusing, sometimes sad, but always astonishing images. And every painting was given a life of its own in the minds of the listeners. He goes past the listeners' heads and directly to their hearts, Mary thought. We learn that what seems meaningless is the only thing that is meaningful.

On their wanderings, they usually slept in a borrowed house belonging to a follower of the new prophet. The first night of the Tyrus journey, they slept in two large rooms in a house belonging to a friend of Levi's. The men spread out their sleeping mats in the larger room, the women in the smaller.

This meant Jesus and Mary Magdalene could not sleep together, so as always in those circumstances, they both woke early and went for a walk together in the surroundings.

'I thought a great deal last night,' Mary said that morning. 'Perhaps the God you speak of has not yet been born in our hearts. That you are far ahead of the rest of us . . . ?'

He shook his head. 'In every man and woman I see into, God is in the core, clearest of all in the wretched, the sick.'

'But if we don't know where God is, it becomes so difficult to seek him.'

'That's so sad, Mary, but he grows slowly in every human being. And one day He will be ready for redemption.'

'Which will be difficult.'

'Yes, all the old must be cast out.'

Mary's flow of memories ceased as she sat in her bed in Antioch. Did they ever get to Tyrus? She didn't know. Had she been able to see the sea? She couldn't remember.

All her images from their wanderings had disappeared into the black despair eclipsing her mind.

29

While Mary was writing down her memories of that winter in Bethsaida and the wandering to Tyrus, she thought carefully over what she should say to the three apostles. And what she should leave out.

Not a word about the Syrian's house, only that Jesus was able to rest during the winter rains. And she had looked after him, cooked his food, and washed and mended his clothes.

She smiled at the memory of how she had struggled with mending his mantle that was always being torn by people who clutched at it to receive some of his strength. Oh well, she thought as she cobbled the rips together. But when they returned to Capernaum, Susanna had taken it over, shaken her head, and had done the mending again.

They were sitting in the pergola as usual. It was a cool day and they almost enjoyed feeling slightly cold.

'According to all testimonies we have collected,' said Paul, 'you and he were often together on your own. There must be words he said to you others do not know.'

She told them about the nightmares she had had that winter and about her terrible fear.

'In the morning I went to him with the dream, hoping he would say that dreams are nothing but soap bubbles that evaporate in the clear light of day. But he didn't. He said the dream was a message from my innermost essence and they knew more than I did. But that I, like most people, isolated myself from the core in which God has his abode within us.'

Paul signed to Marcus to write this down; it was important.

'Later on the wanderings to Tyrus, I asked him whether it could be that the essence he spoke of had still not been born in human beings. That he was perhaps the first on earth who possessed knowledge of God's presence in his own heart. He replied that he could see it in every person. And clearest of all in the sick and those weighed down by guilt.'

There was a long silence while Marcus wrote, then Paul spoke again. 'You didn't ask why he thought that the sick and the tormented had a better knowledge of their . . . real essence?'

'No, it never struck me to.'

Peter came to her aid. 'It's hard to explain why we didn't ask more. It wasn't that we were afraid to, but rather that every answer we were given was so surprising, we had to have time to digest it.'

'Yes, that's what it was,' said Mary.

Then turning to Paul, she said: 'All the same, I think I can answer your question about why he saw the light of God so clearly in the sick and the tormented. That's connected with something else he said.'

She paused to think.

'He said that for us to be aware of the presence of God within us, we had to discard a great deal. All the ideas we build our lives on, all dogmas. All our feeble pride and, perhaps hardest of all, our guilt and our shortcomings.

'He said that the birth of God in our hearts occurs during great pain.'

Paul nodded. Marcus wrote.

Barnabas asked a question. 'How are we to manage that?'

'But he's said that himself – "I am with you always . . ."'

'You're right,' said Paul, who was deeply moved. 'I no longer live without Jesus in me now.'

Mary thought for a moment, then turned to Simon Peter. 'Simon Peter, you ought to know whether Aramaic has a word or two for faith.'

'Only one.'

'Greek has two. Faith and trust. Perhaps it was trust Jesus was speaking about when he said, "Your trust has helped you."'

'Is there any difference?' asked Paul.

Mary laughed briefly before answering. 'I imagine so.'

After a long silence, Mary went on.

'I don't remember much about our wandering to the coast. I was numbed with unease. But what I did observe acquired a new clarity. I actually seemed to understand how his miracles were performed. He made time cease.'

'But my dear Mary,' said Barnabas. 'No one can make time stand still.'

Mary smiled. 'Yes, he could, Barnabas,' she said. 'He met a tormented person, looked into his essence which is of eternity. There the two met, in complete presence. And the miracle could occur. Do you understand?'

She went on after another long silence. 'I remember thinking that it is this presence that is love.'

'Do you mean that what distinguished him from all others was his ability to stop time?'

'Oh, Barnabas, how you do take everything literally. What distinguished him from us was that he was aware that he was in God and God in him. Peter, you must remember how he talked about light, that he who has the light does not submit it to the grain weigher. He meant that it is what we do, we have the insight, but we hide it, we give it no chance to shine through.'

'You've said that he spoke about hearing the voice of God. Now you're talking about the light.'

'But he was always looking for new images to get us to understand. I don't believe he literally spoke about a voice that said ordinary words. I remember asking him once at the beginning how he could be sure that his inner voice was God's. He answered quite simply: "I know."'

30

Terentius and Cipa had gone to a meeting of the Gnostic congregation, so Leonidas and Mary had a simple evening meal in the kitchen. Mary had little appetite and Leonidas was worried when he saw how pale and tired she was.

'I'm worn out,' she said.

It was unlike Mary to complain. Like everyone else in Antioch, he was afraid that after a long hot summer like this one, the plague might strike the town with disease and death.

'Have you a fever?'

'No, I'm just tired.'

She went to bed early and Leonidas sat with her until he was sure she was asleep.

It's too much for her, he thought uneasily, and he decided to stay at home the next day when the apostles were due to come again.

Mary was pleased. She took a long rest in the morning and did nothing but take a stroll in the garden.

'My mind is blank today,' she said. 'It's one of those blessed moments when whims and strange thoughts are silent.'

But her unease took hold the hour before the apostles were due to return. As they sat down in the pergola, Mary had to restrain her inclination to hold Leonidas' hand.

The atmosphere was not as usual. The Greek's presence caused the apostles to put on their masks of pride and dignity. They talked about their difficulties in bringing together all the new things in Jesus' teaching and giving it some kind of definite shape.

Leonidas smiled at Mary. 'I can see your brothers here want you to be more specific. They want facts.'

'But you know Jesus' message can't be stuffed into facts.'

'But that doesn't stop the apostles needing just that.'

147

Mary could almost hear Jesus laughing. She was now in the same situation he had been in, but she did not have his ability to put indisputable, exciting, and important images into words.

But Paul wanted her to be specific. 'They say that during his wanderings all around Tyrus, to a Canaan woman seeking a cure for her daughter, Jesus said that he had not been sent to anyone except the lost sheep of the people of Israel. And that he couldn't take the bread from the children and give it to the dogs.'

Mary's cheeks flared with indignation. 'That's not true,' she cried. 'I was there. I know. It was the woman who spoke those words. She was desperate and probably thought that if she humbled herself with her talk of dogs begging for crumbs at the rich man's table, she would persuade him. But he was filled with compassion and said what he usually said: "O woman, great is your faith." '

Mary looked at the men sitting around her and she stopped at Peter. 'You know he could never have said such a thing! He spoke to the Samaritan woman at the well for a long time and paid her great attention. He received the Greek Leonidas like a brother. He didn't hesitate for a moment to go into the Roman officer's house in Capernaum to cure a sick servant. It was the Roman who stopped him. "Speak the word only, my servant shall be healed." '

Simon Peter said nothing, so Mary went on, slapping her hand on the table. 'You know perfectly well he never differentiated between women and men, heathens and Jews.'

Barnabas came to Simon's rescue. 'Mary, you can't deny that Israel was predestined to become the cradle of Christ.'

'And to become his executioner, according to what is increasingly often said now.'

That was Rabbi Amasya, his voice icy.

'I have also heard that Pilate was himself guided by a crowd of Jews,' said Leonidas. 'But that's so stupid, no one will believe it. Do you think a Roman governor would let himself be influenced by a screaming mob? Jesus was condemned as an agitator after a Roman trial and sentenced to crucifixion, a punishment only the Romans use.'

Simon Peter spoke up. 'It is said that Pilate washed his hands.'

'By all the gods!' cried Leonidas. 'I know Pontius Pilate. He's cruel, cold, and ruthless. A Roman of the worst kind. He loathes the Jews. Would he have appealed to a Jewish mob to spare the life of a mad Jew? That's insane,' he went on, banging on the table. 'Can you imagine a Roman consul washing his hands because he had sentenced a Jew to death? Anyhow, that hand-washing is a Jewish custom that Pilate had scarcely even heard of.'

The silence in the pergola was now thunderous, almost impenetrable.

After a long pause, Leonidas spoke again. 'I realize there is bound to be lively myth making around Jesus. But sometimes it seems to be taking on distasteful expressions. Like the virgin birth.'

'I never speak of it,' said Paul. 'But I know the legend flourishes in many circles.'

Barnabas took over. 'Mary, did you ever hear him speak of his origins?'

'No. He once said his father, Joseph, was a good and right-minded man. But he also said he didn't know him.'

She thought for a moment, then went on, her voice hesitant.

'But something else happened, something that . . . when I was talking to his mother, she told me she was only fifteen when Jesus was born . . . then she looked away, remembering something, I'm sure. But she closed in on herself again and then went on to say that she had never understood her son.'

'Maybe a man walked past her house,' said Leonidas.

The apostles looked frightened.

'How would you summarize his moral message?' Barnabas said to Leonidas.

'His teaching was largely based on ancient wisdom. But he conveyed his message in such an astounding way, he opened up a new reality.'

'What do you mean by ancient wisdom?'

'Moses' message, which has many similarities to the laws of Hammurabi. Not to mention the ancient Egyptians. Do you know what the dead man was to say to Osiris when he met his god in the kingdom of the dead? Mary, you have such a good memory, you can quote . . .'

She hesitated for a moment, then said: 'I can probably remember it in broad outline: "Lord of Truth, before Thee I convey the truth . . . I have annihilated the evil within me . . . I have never killed, nor caused any tears. I have not let any go hungry, nor made any afraid, nor spoken in a haughty voice to call attention to my name. And I have never turned away God in his revelation."'

'Mary,' said Barnabas. 'Are you a Jew or a heathen?'

Mary met his gaze quite calmly. 'I am Christian. Christened by the Master himself.'

Rabbi Amasya and Leonidas smiled. Mary turned to Simon Peter. 'Why must it be a dream in which God said to you that there were no unclean animals in his creation, for you to bring yourself to go to Cornelius, the Roman, who needed to hear about Jesus?'

Peter did not understand the question. 'But you had Jesus' command, didn't you? "Go you therefore, teach all nations . . ."'

Peter hesitated, then said: 'It's a difficult step to take for a Jew. But I obey now. I go around the world and take his word to the heathens.'

'Do you never think about the fact that you're the only people in the world to divide people into believers and heathens?' said Leonidas.

As they said nothing, Leonidas persisted. 'Naturally everyone is imprinted like a coin with the ideas they were brought up with. But you are the only ones to maintain that you alone have the truth. That's hard to understand.'

'We have God's word for it. And we are chosen by him,' said Barnabas.

Leonidas sighed.

Up to then Paul had signalled to Marcus to take down every word that had been said, but now he stiffened and turned to Mary.

'At our very first meeting, you blamed Peter for shutting out those you call Jesus' women disciples. But Simon Peter's task would have been impossible if he had sent women out to convey Jesus' message.'

'Why?' said Mary.

'You know perfectly well the laws say that a woman may only receive instruction in stillness and always submit herself. I shall never allow a woman to convey our teachings.'

'Why not?'

'Because God created Adam first. And because it was woman who was tempted by the serpent and beguiled the man.'

Leonidas and Mary were speechless. They looked at each other.

Rabbi Amasya was upset. 'Somewhere else in the scriptures,' he said, 'it says that God created man in his own image. "Male and female created he them."'

He turned to Leonidas, who replied: 'There's a Jewish philosophical theology and in that, philosophy is a female being. The Book of Proverbs contains the story of Sophia, the daughter of God, who was created long before Man, and who visits the earth to persuade us to listen, and learn.'

He drew a deep breath before going on.

'It has often struck me that her message bears a great resemblance to what Jesus said.'

Paul's reply was short and curt. 'You're quoting from the holy scriptures about which I know but little.'

'But you are learned in the scriptures, a Pharisee,' said Leonidas in astonishment. 'Anyhow, you've decided to follow the message of the Master and go out among all nations.'

Then he went on. 'I know a great deal about your achievements, Paul, more than you think. As far as I can make out, you often form your successful congregations with the aid of free and independent women. We have Lydia in Philippi, Damaris in Athens, and Priscilla the cornerstone of the congregation in Corinth. We have another Priscilla in Rome and yet another Lydia in Thyatira. And that's just a few.'

'One has to take what is there wherever one goes,' said Paul, but he had been cut to the quick.

'I also know,' Leonidas went on, 'that you have had trouble with the congregation in Corinth. There are women there who think they are envoys of philosophy, and the life and acts of Jesus are seen there as a continuation of Sophia's teaching.'

Paul's face was quite closed and it was clear he had no intention of answering, so Leonidas went on. 'Even more important should be that Jesus himself did not regard women as lower beings. Peter, do you remember what he once preached?'

'You mean when he said men should be like women and women like men?' said Peter reluctantly.

He was silent for a while, as if thinking it over, then he sighed and went on. 'I didn't understand it then, nor do I now.'

'And yet it isn't difficult,' said Leonidas sarcastically. 'But I'll stop talking now. No one can argue with prejudices.'

Barnabas paled with anger and answered with a question. 'And which prejudices do you have, adherent that you are of Zeus and all his horrible idols?'

Leonidas laughed. 'I have never joined the cult of Zeus. Anyhow, you've misunderstood the Greek world of gods, which is much more symbolic that you Jews think. I am like Mary now,

Christian, and very critical if you allow yourselves to be caught in old dogmas.'

Mary filled her guests' goblets. They drank despite the dispute, and they parted in a friendly atmosphere. It occurred to Leonidas that Jews loved discussion and splitting hairs, one of their more admirable traits, he thought with some reluctance.

As Paul parted from Mary at the gate, he said: 'One day you must tell us what you saw on Ascension Day. And about his death.'

Mary closed her eyes.

'Do you still mourn him? After all these years?'

'Yes.'

On their way back to the synagogue, Barnabas said, 'She wants us to renounce.'

Rabbi Amasya replied, 'As far as I understand it, that is just what the Master wanted.'

Paul took no part in the conversation, absorbed as he was in the question of how Leonidas could know so much about his congregations in the Greco-Roman world. And first and foremost, how could the Greek know about the internal antagonisms in Corinth?

One day I'll ask him and he will answer me.

31

'Let's take a walk in the garden before dinner.'

The suggestion came from Leonidas when Mary returned to the pergola. She nodded and smiled.

'You mean we need to calm down?'

Leonidas laughed. 'No, I was neither surprised nor upset.'

They walked up the winding path to the highest terrace, where they looked out over the sea and watched the sun disappearing.

'Now that we're alone, there's something else I want to draw your attention to,' said Leonidas. 'Have you noticed that Terentius keeps appearing during our talks with the apostles? He shows nothing and is as courteous as always, but his ears are burning with curiosity.'

Mary looked so surprised that Leonidas had to laugh at her. Then he quickly turned serious when he saw her blush. 'Have no fear,' he said hurriedly. 'He's loyal and he's never indiscreet. That's gone into the marrow of his bones.'

'I'm not afraid,' she said. 'But ashamed. It occurs to me that I've been taking Terentius and his wife entirely for granted in my home. No longer as human beings. That's terrible.'

Leonidas was surprised. 'He has created the distance, not you.'

She said nothing. It was true. But Jesus would never have approved and would have forced a confrontation.

'When I purchased those two from Livia,' said Leonidas, 'she said in passing that the only thing she had against Terentius was that he and his wife belonged to some secret Christian sect.'

Mary was speechless with surprise.

'You must see,' Leonidas went on, 'what an impression it made on him when he found out you were Mary Magdalene. There are sects in Antioch to which you are almost as holy as Jesus himself.'

Mary stood still as she gazed over the town and thought about how she had walked along the great avenues and listened to the Buddhist monks in their saffron yellow robes and heard the Zoroastrian wise men preaching. In Antioch, she had found Iranian thinking on the resurrection of the soul, Jewish philosophy, Babylonian astrology, and Greek philosophy. She had increasingly often stopped at the Indian wise men and listened to them speaking of the core of man being identical with

God, even recognized it – Jesus could have said the same, although his words would have been different.

But she had never heard of any secret Christian sects. So they existed, did they?

By the time Leonidas had gone into his office the next morning, she had made a decision. She intercepted Terentius on his way to the market and said firmly: 'I want to talk to you.'

His expression remained unchanged until she asked him to sit down opposite her desk in the library. His handsome olive-coloured face darkened, and Mary found an opening for their conversation.

'I understand you and I have the same Master. Everyone has the same value before Jesus. If you insist on remaining standing, then I'll do the same.'

She rose, stood as upright as a statue, her arms folded, then suddenly noticed his mouth twitching, and with some astonishment reckoned he was almost smiling.

He sat down. So did she.

'Tell me about your faith, Terentius,' she said.

It was an order, and her tone of voice surprised her. But it had the desired effect. The Nubian began haltingly to describe the Gnostic congregation in Antioch. He told her about the road to knowledge that went to the innermost of man and which could not be taught. Mary listened and when he stopped, said, 'Do you think you could take me with you to one of your services?'

'Yes.'

'As you must know, I have to guard my anonymity.'

'I know. But there would be no risk. You can take your black cloak and keep your face veiled. If anyone asks, I will say you are a . . . friend and a seeker. This evening after dark.'

'Good,' said Mary. 'And thank you for talking to me.'

He backed to the door.

It was a large room in a wealthy household. They sat on cushions on the floor and there were many people there, slaves and free, men and women together. Many of them greeted Terentius and his wife warmly, and no one asked who the veiled woman with them was. The atmosphere was solemn, though the service was introduced with a lottery. Surprised, Mary realized that they were drawing lots for who should lead the service, who should take on the role of priest and preach, who should give the sacrament and who should lead the prayer.

'No definite hierarchy is allowed,' whispered Terentius when he saw Mary's surprise. 'All are equal here.'

A woman took the part of priest. She was not young, the years and experience etching wrinkles into her face, but she was slender and tall, her clothing a brilliant red.

'We who have renounced the demiurge know that the power the naive worship as Creator and Almighty is nothing but an image,' she began. 'The true God is not King and Lord. It is not he who makes the laws, demanding revenge and leading us into bloody wars.'

She kept moving all the time she was preaching, her arms speaking in great gestures, her feet moving as if in a dance. Then she stood stock still for a moment.

'Gnosis is to acquire insight into the true source, namely the depths in everything that is. All those who have learned to know this source have learned to know themselves.'

Mary's heart thumped. The woman went on.

'The apostles are now spreading the word of the resurrection of the body of Jesus. But we know he is spirit and with us in all our actions. We also know that we must rise from the dead while we are alive. Those who say that we must first die and then rise in the perished body are preaching false doctrines.'

Mary hesitated. She could hear those words on the grain of wheat: 'Except a corn of wheat fall into the ground and die . . .'

'We know that after his crucifixion Christ appeared to certain disciples in visions. First and foremost to Mary Magdalene. At a troubled meeting in Jerusalem, she told them what he had said to her.'

Mary could only occasionally take in the way the woman on the podium repeated word for word what she had once said. It had been preserved! Someone had remembered . . . tears blinded her, the veil over her face making breathing difficult and she was sweating under her heavy cloak.

The rest of the service passed her by. When Terentius and his wife went up to receive the bread and wine, she walked slowly down the steps and out onto the street, where she drew a deep breath of the cool night air.

The three of them walked home in silence, Mary hoping Leonidas would be back. But he had not returned, and as if in a trance, she went to her room, took off her clothes, and lay down on her bed.

I'll never sleep, she thought.

The next moment, she was asleep.

She woke at dawn, burdened, and she went into Leonidas' room and ruthlessly shook him awake.

'I have to talk to you.'

She told him and he listened.

'You've been drawn into a game which is far greater than we thought,' he said.

'What game?'

'It's all about power, about the power the new church is to be based on.'

He said nothing for a while as he sat there in bed. Then he said: 'Don't let yourself be exploited by anyone. I beg you, Mary. Keep away from all sects, Peter's and Paul's as well.'

32

After breakfast that same morning, when Leonidas had gone to the merchant house, Mary went to speak to Terentius. He was sweeping the courtyard. 'May we have a word?'

He brushed down his clothes and followed her into the pergola.

'Sit down.'

'I'd rather stand.'

Mary sighed and went on.

'You no doubt realize it was a great . . . experience for me to take part in your service. Do you know from where you acquired the information on . . . the dispute in Jerusalem?'

'No.'

'Do you think I could meet the woman who was preaching?'

He looked troubled. 'I suppose that could be arranged,' he said. 'But would it be wise? She's a quick thinker and she would soon know who you are.'

Mary realized he was right.

'If you like,' said Terentius. 'I could keep you informed on what happens with the Gnostics.'

'I'd be grateful. Who is the demiurge?'

'The god the Jews believe in,' he said. 'We consider him a fallen angel constantly battling with God.'

'That's strange teaching.'

Terentius did not reply, bowed and made to leave. But Mary stopped him.

'Why does your wife never say anything?'

If he flushed, she could not see it in his dark face, but she suddenly understood what Leonidas had meant when he spoke of Terentius' burning ears. The Nubian hesitated, then spoke.

'Cipa was sold at the age of seven to a brothel in Thebes. She was raped and tortured for months. But she screamed all the time, so they wearied of her, cut out her tongue, and threw her out on the street. That's where I found her.'

Mary quickly rose, went past Terentius and out into the kitchen, where Cipa was preparing vegetables. She went straight over to the girl and took her in her arms.

They stood there for a long time, then both of them wept.

Exhausted, Mary did something unusual for her; she went to her bedroom and lay down on the bed.

Her head felt heavy and her mind was in a whirl, her thoughts scattered and inconclusive. She tried praying, but could not do that, either.

The next moment she was asleep and dreaming – a dark room on the upper floor of a large house in Jerusalem, Jesus asleep at her side. She woke from someone banging on the door. Even in her dream, she felt herself resisting – she had no desire to go back to Jerusalem, not now, not yet.

But the dream went on.

She heard Andrew, who was on night watch, speaking. But the other voice was used to giving orders, clearly and demandingly. That woke Jesus, who called down the stairs.

'Tell him I'm coming.'

As he drew his mantle over his tunic, he turned to Mary. 'It's Nicodemus,' he said. 'One of the councillors in the Sanhedrin.'

Mary wanted to tell him not to go, but she had learned not to show her fears.

She pulled on her mantle, too, slipped a little way down the stairs and sat down. She knew Jesus could see her, as could Andrew on guard by the door.

The man's voice was more respectful now. 'We know you come from God. No one can make the signs you do if God is not with him.'

Jesus' reply surprised Mary. 'Except a man be born again, he cannot see the kingdom of God.'

Nicodemus showed his surprise. 'How can a man be born

when he is old? Can he enter the second time into his mother's womb and be born?'

'Verily, I say unto you, except a man be born again, he cannot see the kingdom of God. Except a man be born again, he cannot be born of water and the spirit, he cannot enter the kingdom of heaven. That which is born of the flesh is flesh; and that which is born of the spirit is spirit. Marvel not that I said unto you, You must be born again. The wind bloweth where it listeth, and you hearest the sound thereof, but canst not tell whence or whither it goeth. So is everyone that is born of the spirit.'

A moment later, she saw the tall man in the tufted cloak disappearing.

As the door closed again, Mary woke in her bed in Antioch, clear-minded and sure. She took a bath, washed her hair, and put on clean clothes. Then she sat in the garden, letting the sun dry her flowing hair. It was warm, but a cool wind was sweeping in from the sea.

The wind bloweth where it listeth, Mary thought, closing her eyes and remembering.

Part Three

33

They crossed the lake by boat, then headed for Jericho. Mary was feeling lighthearted, an unexpected joy, as for a while her great unease had left her.

Her eyes were as clear as a child's and she could see as never before, trees budding, anemones in the newly-cut grass, the lilies in the ground neither sowing nor harvesting, but simply glowing with the joy of themselves, God, and people.

'And the turtle is heard in our land . . .'

They were walking in the valley of the river Jordan, occasionally glimpsing the river, sometimes taking a rest on the banks and washing their dusty feet in the fast-flowing water. But the further south they went, the harder it became to get down to the river, the undergrowth impenetrable, a mass of acacias, sharp thorns, and numerous kinds of reeds. Aromatic rushes. And papyrus covering the shores and continuing far out into the water.

An hour or two later, the air was full of aromas. Mary stopped and sniffed. Levi saw her amazement and said: 'It's balsam, one of the trees that made Jericho famous.' Then, almost taking them by surprise, the oasis appeared before them, a shimmering mirage, greener than any place Mary had ever seen, but also with pink almond blossoms, red with roses, and golden with broom. Mary was filled with wonder.

Tall trunks with no low foliage lined the road, their huge crowns high up in the sky.

'They're date palms,' said Levi.

They could now see the great crowds that had gathered along

the road in expectation of seeing Jesus. Mary was no longer surprised, for she had learned that it was not only his reputation that went before him. Simon sent out his messengers – no child, man, or woman in Jericho had not been reached by the news that Jesus of Nazareth was to stay at the oasis on his way to Passover in Jerusalem. Many of them knew him, for he had visited them before during his wanderings between the towns of Judea, where he had cured the sick and spoken of the kingdom of God. People from Jerusalem were also there, the lame, the blind.

And a number of scribes.

Mary sighed. She was afraid of disputes and would have liked him to rest after the long walk. But he did as he always did, stopped for the tormented, took their hands in his and gave them cures and new hope.

A blind man called out. 'Jesus, son of David, have mercy on me.'

People tried to silence him, but Jesus went through the crowd and asked the blind man, 'What do you want of me?'

'Do so that I can see again.'

'You can see. Great is your faith.'

The disciples were tired and hungry, but they had to wait many hours before they could go on to the oasis. There was a man sitting up in a sycamore, a small man with long arms and short legs, a big nose but without a hair on his head.

A rich man, but despised by the inhabitants of the town.

Mary understood, as if she at once knew why he had climbed up the tree. He was a head shorter than his neighbours, but had decided that he would see the Master.

She hid a smile.

But Jesus looked up into the tree. 'Make haste, Zacchæus, and come down; for today I must abide at your house.'

As the little man slid down the tree, she could hear a murmur running through the crowd. 'He has gone to be guest with a man who is a sinner.'

When the publican reached the ground, he straightened up and turned to Jesus. 'Behold, Lord, the half of my goods I shall give to the poor; and if I have taken anything from any man by false accusation, I shall restore him fourfold.'

Then he hurried away to prepare the midday meal.

As they went on toward Zacchæus' house, Jesus was stopped by a scribe who asked when the kingdom of God was coming. He replied as usual that the kingdom of God would come in a way that he could see it with his own eyes.

'Neither shall they say, "Lo here!" or "lo there!" The kingdom of God is within you.'

He said it so many times and so clearly, Mary thought, and yet no one understood.

At table in the publican's house, melancholy again overtook Mary and her eyes darkened with anxiety. After their midday rest, she heard Jesus talking to some Pharisees who kept warning him. 'Hurry away from here. Herod wants to kill you.'

But his answer was clear. 'Go you and tell, behold, I cast out devils, and I do cures today and tomorrow and the third day I shall be perfected. Nevertheless I must walk today and tomorrow and the day following, for it cannot be that a prophet perish out of Jerusalem.'

When night fell, they spread out their sleeping mats in Zacchæus' house, the men in the largest room, the women in a smaller one. Mary went to find Lydia, a woman who was new among the disciples. Mary had grown fond of her for her endless patience. Jesus had met her in a synagogue in Galilee, bowed to the ground from an injury to her back and for many years she had been unable to stand upright. Jesus had noticed her, called her to him, put his hands on her and told her she was now free of her ailment.

Mary had many memories of the cured. But this was one of

the clearest. She would never forget Lydia's face as she straightened up, rose to her full height, and drew a deep breath, freed of her torments.

She came to stay with them, gave her savings to the common purse, and spread her wisdom and joy among them all.

She now put her arms around Mary and pulled her to her. She said nothing, but Mary was able to weep.

The next day they went on, followed by great crowds. The landscape changed, the earth less fertile and the bare mountains higher and higher. Although they still had a long way to go, they could see the town, proudly and self-confidently settled on Mount Zion.

Mary detested it from the very first moment. She found it arrogant and enclosed behind its thick walls. A strange thought came to her – a world without cracks can never be found behind walls.

The town was dominated by the enormous temple that caught the rays of the sun and threw them back in golden reflections across the valley.

Many of the followers fell to their knees at the sight. 'Mighty, mighty is the God of Israel.' But Mary stayed standing, thinking that this god was a different god from Jesus', who spoke with those who spoke with the great Abba.

She looked at the Master. His eyes were wide open and the sweat was pouring off his forehead. The sweat of anguish?

Jesus and his disciples turned off toward the valley of Cedron before reaching the town wall, then went up the steep road over the Mount of Olives and continued to Bethany, to the house of Martha and Mary.

Mary Magdalene had heard the story of Jesus bringing the dead Lazarus back to life. Now she was to meet him. He had strange eyes, his gaze fixed in the far distance. She wanted to talk to him, ask . . . He was the person who could tell her about death. But he was timid and silent, and avoided them all.

Martha noticed. 'My brother seems still not adjusted to life,' she said.

Mary liked Martha, the housewife who saw to the food for the many who came to table, found sleeping places, and cared for everyone's needs. In her resolute way of doing things, she reminded Mary of Euphrosyne. Her sister Mary was more difficult to fathom, far away from the everyday and dreamily absorbed in Jesus. It irritated Mary Magdalene, but well into the afternoon she admitted to herself that she was jealous.

Mary from Bethsaida was beautiful, pleasing, and shy as Jewish custom prescribed, everything Mary Magdalene had never been.

But when Martha sent them together to the village well to fetch water for the evening meal, Mary Magdalene happened to meet Mary's eyes and at once saw that she knew and was miserable and afraid. They stood there, recognizing one another.

'Why don't the disciples understand what is going to happen?'
'They don't want to. They deny it.'

The anguish in her was now so strong, Mary in Antioch had to take herself out of her memories.

34

Mary had just begun to write down her memories of Jericho and her meeting in Jerusalem when she heard the gate open and Leonidas calling out to her. He was back early today.

'Come on,' he said. 'Let's take a walk and see Simon Peter laying the foundation stone of the first church.'

Mary knew the new Christian congregation had been given land next to the town wall where the old synagogue had once been. That had burned down many years ago and the site had been cleared over the summer.

So the time to lay the cornerstone had come.

She drew the veil over her face and threw her black cloak over her shoulders.

There were a lot of people at the site where Peter was reading the simple prayer Jesus had taught them, blessing the site and asking the Master to protect the new church building. Paul was standing next to Simon, also sunk in prayer.

Rabbi Amasya was on the edge of the crowd, so Leonidas pulled Mary with him and they went over to him.

'I think we need to talk to you, Rabbi.'

She was pleased. This was what she wanted. And Rabbi Amasya said he would come to their house after the evening meal.

They waited for the rabbi in the library. Mary lit the two big oil lamps and put fruit on the table. She was having doubts now. She no longer wanted to talk to anyone about the events of those last few days. When the rabbi sat down in the guest chair, her resistance was so great, she pressed her lips together so that her mouth became a thin line.

Rabbi Amasya was not put off. He was worried.

'It was incautious of you to go to the Gnostic service,' he said. 'Rumours are buzzing around now – who was the mysterious woman and what did she want of them? The fanciful maintain she was the angel of darkness sent there to spy on them. But some whisper about the apostle surpassing all others, the woman who according to the Gnostics "was given the knowledge of the Universe". A man came to me today and asked me straight out whether the merchant Leonidas was married to Mary Magdalene.'

'I know it was incautious,' said Mary, but her voice was curt and very firm as she went on. 'I have no regrets. It was good to hear them and see their order of service. A woman was preaching and said that Gnosis is to come to insight of the true source, namely the depths in everything that is. All those who learned of this source have done so by themselves. I recognized it. The words were not Jesus', but the meaning . . .'

Rabbi Amasya shook his head. 'I'm not talking about their teaching. There's a lot of good in it. What I'm trying to warn you about is what happens if you come forward. You'll be surrounded by zealots and worshipped as the apostle who has the only truth. That is a difficult role not suited to you, Mary. You have constantly distanced yourself from authorities, and you might become one yourself.'

It was quite quiet in the library now, and they could hear the wind going through the high trees in the garden.

'It's true, Rabbi,' Leonidas said finally. 'Mary wouldn't have a quiet moment if it became known who she was. She is making her contribution here in the library. And her writings will still be here when the bickering between the various Christian sects has long been forgotten.'

They were right, Mary thought, but she also felt defiant. Not even Leonidas understood that sometimes she seemed to be living in a vacuum.

I was chosen, after all, she thought.

But she said nothing.

Amasya and Leonidas went on talking about the Gnostics. The rabbi said the multiplicity of Gnostic faith was so great that there was nothing secure and proven to hold on to.

'The individual's inner route to God has many pitfalls,' he went on. 'So, for instance, Gnostics were unable to tell the difference between visions and reality. Anyone can have a revelation and then incorporate it into his teaching, adding to it and taking away as he wishes. Peter is right in that in the same way as Judaism, Christianity has to have a firm faith with definite doctrines so people all over the world can always go back to one and the same truth.'

Mary said nothing. So multiplicity was to be a bad thing, she thought. Jesus himself had said to her: 'Write no laws . . .'

But that was only in a vision.

The two men went on talking and Mary stopped listening. Not until Rabbi Amasya rose to leave did she ask a question. 'Why don't you join Christianity?'

He flushed and she realized she had gone too far. But he was an honest man, so sat down again as he sought for an honest answer. 'It's because I'm so firmly anchored in the Jewish faith. Like all orthodox Jews, I am awaiting the Messiah, the king who is to come to power and glory and free the Jewish people.'

He was speaking to Leonidas, although Mary had asked the question. The Greek looked surprised and disappointed and Rabbi Amasya flung out his hands, suddenly voluble, 'You must understand that I cannot reconcile that dream with a barefoot preacher from Galilee who allows himself to be executed as a criminal.'

Mary wanted to say that Jesus wore sandals, but she restrained herself, and said instead: 'How is he then to come? On clouds from the Jewish god of hosts to destroy all other peoples?'

Rabbi Amasya remained deep in thought for a while, then spoke again. 'He had power, this Jesus, that appears from your descriptions. But what use did he put it to? Curing a few hundred suffering people of their diseases and torments. A few hundred out of the suffering millions of the world. What use was that? Reducing the suffering – did that do anything to the basic conditions? Isn't evil as great as ever? And injustices and suffering? That he spoke fair words is nothing new. Israel has had plenty of preachers who have made themselves into interpreters of what is largely the same message.'

They sat in silence.

'Why were his deeds so small?' the rabbi cried. 'He had the power. He shouldn't have spent hours over a few individual people.'

'But that was where his greatness lay. Can't you see that it was in this meeting, person to person, that the new was born. A new vision, a new way. I have heard you say there is only one way of serving God and that is to see him in every beggar.'

Rabbi Amasya groaned and was about to protest, but Mary stopped him.

'Listen,' she said. 'What would the Messiah achieve with mighty acts? New conditions for some and new suffering for others. A new rebellion, new wretchedness, new wars.'

She leaned forward and went on, emphasizing every word. 'What Jesus taught us was to see and love and care for every single person. That was what was new.'

Rabbi Amasya again tried to explain, but Leonidas interrupted him. 'I don't understand you. It is as Mary says. What would happen if your Messiah came and created a new Jewish realm on earth? Bloody slaughter of those you call heathens. And after a while, the conquered people would rise and take bloody revenge.'

'I'm talking about the kingdom of god,' said Rabbi Amasya, but his voice had lost its resonance.

'And what is that?'

'A kingdom that is not of this world.'

'Do you know who said those words?'

'No.'

'It was Jesus.'

'I didn't know that,' said Rabbi Amasya.

When Mary went to bed that night, she thought she had at last understood why Peter and the others had not listened when Jesus spoke of his degradation and death. The image of the Jewish Messiah was incompatible with the fate Jesus walked straight into with his eyes open and in great anguish.

Just as she was falling asleep, she heard the cry from Golgotha: 'He saved others; himself he cannot save.'

171

And the mocking laughter.

She sat up, struck by a thought. Was that perhaps what he had wanted with the crucifixion? To show how whoever has power is able to decline to use it?

Other words appeared: 'Take up your cross and follow me.'

The next morning she was back in Bethany outside Jerusalem.

35

They were given an abundant evening meal in Bethany. Martha served them, pressing the food on them. Jesus smiled at her from the table where he lay with Mary Magdalene at his side.

Lazarus partook in the meal, but his gaze was far away and he ate practically nothing. Mary noticed that that worried Jesus.

Her own attention was on Martha's sister, the young Mary, whose hands shook so much she was unable to touch the food. She was staring, unseeing, across the table, her eyes dark and unnaturally large, then she suddenly got up and ran to her room in the inner part of the house and came back with a flask made of expensive glass. When she opened it, the air was filled with the fragrance of spikenard. She knelt down and began to anoint Jesus' feet with the precious oil.

When she was done, she dried his feet on her hair.

They could hear people gathering in the courtyard, people from Jerusalem who wanted to hear Jesus. But exhausted as he was, he shook his head. After saying grace, he took Mary Magdalene's hand and they went out into the garden at the back.

The flowers had all died and thistles and briars had taken over. Mary reckoned no one in the house had had the strength to weed or water since Lazarus had fallen ill.

They sat down on a bench by the wall. A piercing wind was whistling around the house, penetrating their clothes and even their skin. She had heard of these desert winds that blew through the body and drove all hope from people's souls.

He was still holding her hand, but his was cold and his grip feeble. 'We are to say farewell to each other now,' he said.

She wanted to cry out no, that she was going to follow him all the long way to death, but her voice had gone. He smiled, a smile full of tenderness and despair.

Then he said that he did not want her and the other women to be with him during these last days. 'What soldiers do to women is worse than death,' he said.

Then he told her about the man with the water jar who owned a house in Jerusalem. He would look after the women disciples, hide and protect them.

'As soon as possible, I shall come there to see you.'

Then he went on: 'You're not safe even here in Bethany. The resurrected Lazarus is a dangerous witness.'

Mary did not understand the connection, but now she was able to whisper: 'I suppose we can follow at a distance?'

'Yes, mix in the crowds that will be around me. But don't reveal yourselves.'

He was gazing into the thorny thicket in the neglected garden, and when he again looked into her face, she saw he was weeping.

'You know that I am with you always.'

With an effort, Mary Magdalene pushed away the memory of the neglected garden and that terrible wind. She rose from her chair in the pergola in Antioch, her voice now restored and trembling with anger.

'With me always! The truth is that you follow me only like a whisper in the wind. It blows where it likes, and like a

173

presentiment in the air when things are at their hardest. But that's not enough, not enough.'

She had a raging headache and decided to rest for a while. As she lay back on her bed, her head pressed into the pillow, she thought – God in heaven, why is it not enough for me?

She tried to sleep, but the images in her memory returned at full strength the moment she closed her eyes.

36

The sun was above Bethany as they assembled for morning prayers the next day. The fierce wind had subsided and Jesus prayed for them.

'Holy Father, keep through thine own name, those whom you have given me, that they may be one, as we are. I kept them in your name: those that you gavest me, I have kept, and none of them is lost but the son of perdition.

'They do not belong in the world, just as I do not belong in the world. As thou hast sent me to the world, I have sent them.' As he went on, he seemed to turn directly to the women. 'You shall weep and lament, but the world shall rejoice: you shall be sorrowful, but your sorrow shall be turned to joy. A woman when she is in travail, because her hour has come: but as soon as she has been delivered of the child, she remembereth no more the anguish, for joy that a man is born into the world. And you now have sorrow but I shall see you again and you shall rejoice and your joy no man shall take from you.'

The men prepared for the walk to the town. Jesus rode on a donkey and in the distance the women could see the people waiting for him. Thousands of people tore branches from the trees and strewed them in his path, others spread out their mantles. When the women came nearer, they could hear the cries from those ahead and those behind.

'Hosanna: Blessed is the King of Israel that cometh in the name of the Lord.'

High above all the voices, they could hear Simon Peter's as he cried out:

'Blessed is our Father's Kingdom of David.'

Mary Magdalene covered her mouth to stop herself from crying out. Keep quiet. The other women were also frightened. This was a challenge and would not be forgiven.

When the women had reached the grove on the slopes of the Mount of Olives, they stopped to rest, sitting in the shade of the old trees and watching the jubilant procession of thousands disappearing through the city gate on its way toward the temple.

Mary told them what Jesus had said of the dangers that might threaten the women and the necessity to keep at a distance from him and everything that was now to happen.

Some of them looked relieved. They had known the risks. But Mary crumpled, Mary mother of Jacob and Joseph, her whole body trembling. Lydia sat down beside her, but had no words with which to console her.

In the end, slowly and heavily, they took the road toward the town wall and through the gateway. No one stopped them. They were only a few in the stream of Jewish women and men from all over the world, come to sacrifice a lamb in the holy city.

The alleys were seething with people and soldiers. Susanna said quietly that the Roman proconsul had brought a whole army with him to the Passover celebrations in Jerusalem.

'What for?' said Salome, who was frightened of all crowds and all Romans.

'They're afraid there'll be a riot,' whispered Susanna.

Then everything happened just as Jesus had said, a man with a water jar on his shoulder gave them an almost invisible sign and started walking slowly ahead of them.

His house was near the wall, large and well equipped, enclosed by heavy gates on to the street. He showed them up the stairs to the first floor, where two rooms had been put in order. An elderly Greek servant by the name of Helena received them with warmth, bread, and cheese. She was voluble, in contrast to her husband, who had still not yet opened his mouth. When he finally did, it was to warn them. They were not to walk in a group as when they had come. Whenever they left the house, they must go in pairs and melt into the crowd as soon as possible.

They nodded. That they were in hostile country was clear.

That afternoon, the rumour flew around that Jesus had driven the moneylenders out of the temple. He had tipped over tables, been lashed with a scourge, and had cursed those who made the house of God into Mammon's.

'There may be something in it,' said Helena breathlessly. 'But the pilgrims were waiting outside in long queues to exchange their money. And what are they to do when they can't buy a sacrificial lamb?'

The women cried out in dismay, and some just wept. Only Mary Magdalene stood mute and rigid, knowing that now there was no longer any return.

Toward evening, Helena came back with more terrible rumours. The Romans had crushed a riot in the temple, five zealots had been arrested and taken to Pontius Pilate.

'Zealots?' said Mary in surprise.

'Yes, that's what they call themselves. Others call them the knifemen because they have long knives hidden in their robes.'

Mary remembered one of the disciples, Simon the Zealot. He had come to Jesus after John the Baptist had been killed.

The next morning they went two by two, as the man with the water jar had told them to, out into the alleys toward the temple. They took careful note of the way, worried about not finding their way back − a fat greengrocer on one corner, an awkward stone pillar on another. Nor did they have any difficulty finding

Jesus, for great crowds had surrounded him. They never got near him, for the human wall did not make way for latecomers.

Mary's view was blurred by her tears, for she had longed to see him. But then she heard a voice, a clear young voice that reached them all. 'Is it lawful to give tribute to Caesar, or not?'

Mary was uneasy; that was a dangerous question.

But Jesus' voice was calm, almost laughing, as he replied. 'Show me a dinar. Whose image and name is on it?'

'Caesar's,' cried the people.

'Render to Caesar the things that are Caesar's, and to God the things that are God's,' Jesus said.

The people laughed and Mary and Lydia smiled at each other.

I must have some more memories of those days in the temple, Mary thought as she sat in her garden in Antioch. But a layer of black soot seemed to have settled over her senses there in Jerusalem. She could recall no clear memories.

Yes – one.

On one of those long days, she and Susanna happened to come across him as he sat speaking on a rock. It was early morning, but nevertheless people had gathered around him. Mary did not listen, simply looked at his face and saw how tired and despairing he was, and she realized at last that death was the only thing that could free him.

He was drawing in the sand.

Then a howling group of men suddenly pushed their way up to him, with them a woman who had been taken in adultery.

'The laws prescribe that such women be stoned to death,' they cried loudly. 'What sayest thou?'

Jesus went on drawing in the sand, then after a long silence, looked up. 'He that is without sin among you, let him cast the first stone.'

The enraged men dropped their hands and went away, one by one, and the crowd silently dispersed.

Only the adulteress was left, and Mary and Susanna hiding behind a pillar. They heard Jesus asking the woman: 'Where did they go? Did no one condemn you?'

She whispered her reply. 'No, Lord.'

'Neither do I condemn thee. Go now and sin no more.'

As Jesus rose to leave a little later, his eyes met Mary's. As he walked past the two women, he spoke. 'I shall come to you tonight.'

For a moment she felt the joy almost shattering her. Her face flared, her heart thumped, and her feet ran down the temple steps. They returned to the house, two by two as they had learned, and the other women all brightened when they passed on the message.

Then the long wait for the night, the darkness. For the first time they noticed that the night was never really dark in the town. And never silent. People walked along the streets talking loudly. Roman soldiers marched, and for a long spell they had to listen to a quarrel between two women.

But in the darkest hour, he was there in the big hall. The women wept, silently and abandonedly. They could all see how weary he was. They had prepared a bath and a room with soft bolsters for him.

So they lay there. Her hands felt his body, every muscle of it tense, and her hands suddenly remembered an art she had learned long ago. Gently, she massaged him, his back, his shoulders, arms, and legs.

They did not speak, for there was no longer anything to say.

He slept, soundly and calmly. She must also have slept, but when she was awakened by Nicodemus knocking, her pillow was wet.

After the councillor had left, they could just make out the dawn over the mountains in the east. Jesus kissed her and they both knew it was for the last time. Then he vanished, as unnoticeably as he had come. Mary tried to sleep for a while, but could not.

At breakfast, which the women ate in their room, they started talking about the men, the disciples. Where were they? Susanna had heard that they had gone back to Galilee. Salome said that they had gone up the mountains. Only John and Andrew, who had been with him that night, had stayed.

'How could they be so cowardly?' cried Mary Magdalene. But Mary, mother of Jacob and Joseph, said, 'They say it's now dangerous even to have known him.'

The Greek woman came in while they were talking. 'A woman has come to find you. She says she belongs with you. My husband isn't at home and I don't know what to do.'

They looked at each other.

A woman? Who? Who knew about the house? What did she want of them? Fear made it hard to breathe. Finally Mary Magdalene rose. 'I'll go and see who it is,' she said.

And there she was, the mother of Jesus. 'It is to be done, is it true?'

'Yes.'

Their eyes met in dark despair.

As so often for women, the daily chores provided relief in their anxiety. Mary of Nazareth had walked far that night and she had to wash, be given food, be allowed to sleep. She soon recovered and just said she had so much to ask them.

But one after another, they replied. 'We have no answers.'

In the afternoon, the mother of Jesus and Mary Magdalene went to the temple. The crowd around Jesus was so great, they could only catch a glimpse of him in the distance. Mixing among them all were also councillors from the Sanhedrin, temple guards, and Roman soldiers.

Early next morning there was again a knocking on the door. The man with the water jar was now at home and went to open the door himself. This time it was John, the youngest of the disciples.

His gaze sought Mary Magdalene's. 'They took him at dawn,' he said.

She seemed not to hear him, just stood there thinking about John, for whom she had never felt any sympathy. He had been called Jesus' youngest disciple, was handsome in appearance, and he had a pleasant manner.

The next moment, her thoughts were shattered by the wailing of the women. Slowly, the meaning of John's message sank in. She found it difficult to walk steadily as she went to Mary of Nazareth and they embraced, holding on to each other, neither able to weep.

Mary of Nazareth finally broke the silence. 'Where is he?'

'A captain from the temple guard was there when the Roman soldiers seized him. The temple guard requested that the prisoner first be taken to the Grand Council. So they took him there and Caiaphas interrogated him. No one may know what was said. Then he was led in shackles to Pontius Pilate.'

'What will happen to him?'

The silence was long and heavy.

In the end, Mary Magdalene said, 'They will crucify him.'

37

For the next few hours, Mary Magdalene busied herself with inessentials. Why was Jesus' mother wearing a sky-blue robe? And John, the young boy, why did he have such trouble placing his feet? Did he have to stumble?

She had chosen her most down-at-heel shoes.

Just as they were leaving the house, she felt hungry and asked the Greek woman for a piece of bread, which she then broke into pieces and ate as they walked, two by two, down the alleyways toward the wall, through the gateway, and out to Mount Calvary.

The sun was above Mount Zion.

It was going to be a hot day.

No matter. I am cold.

Mary of Nazareth was swaying in front of her. Mary Magdalene caught up with her and held out her hand, but her hand was strangely feeble, so in a hard voice Mary Magdalene told John he should help the mother of Jesus.

He obeyed but continued stumbling.

When she saw the execution place, even all these meaningless thoughts ceased and she was drained of emotion, flung out of time.

Yet there were some sensible moments. An elderly man came up to them and said he was Joseph of Arimathea and a friend. Then he looked at them for a long time and said in a subdued voice that it was dangerous to stand by the cross, that the Romans had a habit of crucifying those mourning the executed.

Mary Magdalene laughed in his face, then pulled herself together. 'Don't you see,' she said. 'I would like to die with him.'

He stroked her cheek.

Then he said he had a garden nearby with a cave tomb already prepared. He would ask the Romans whether he could take the body to it. Mary Magdalene kept her head, reckoning he would almost certainly have his way, for he was a rich man with great authority.

After a while she was again back in that emptiness, the heat vibrating on the bare rock. Mary was cold, for the first time noticing that her whole body was shaking, but it did not affect her; and with no surprise, she seemed no longer to exist within her body.

Then cries from the mob could be heard, and he was there with his cross, lashed, tortured, the crown of thorns pressed down onto his forehead. Blood was pouring down his face and pieces of flesh peeling from his ravaged back. Both eyes had been blackened and he could see nothing.

Mary Magdalene was then flung out of her emptiness, the pain like knives slicing through her, and she screamed, screamed like a madwoman.

Joseph of Arimathea covered her mouth with his hand and held it there as the soldiers drove the nails through Jesus' hands. She closed her eyes, praying for forgiveness for it, and when she opened them, for a moment she saw the other women with their hands over their ears at the terrible crunching sound.

She closed her eyes again as the cross was raised, but that was no help, the knives slicing through her and twisting around and around inside her, worst of all in her heart, the knife in it burning like fire.

The next moment the blessed emptiness returned and she was not herself, nor did she exist in this place.

The scornful cries rang all around her – 'He saved others; himself he cannot help.' The crowds who had praised him were now absorbing with pleasure his torment and enjoying it. A memory shot through her head – 'Mary, I had no inkling people were so evil.'

She glanced at the mother of Jesus and saw Joseph putting his arm around her. Then the other crosses were raised, two more men to be executed. She looked up at one of them. He had been less severely tortured than Jesus and he defiantly returned her gaze. She recognized him, she knew him.

But when, where had she met him?

He spoke to Jesus and Jesus answered him, but no one on the ground heard what he said.

The hours crawled by, time without end. At the sixth hour,

the sky darkened, the terrible wind from the deserts swept over the town, into people's lungs, tormenting them. She hoped the desert sand would fill his body and cut short his suffering.

But he did not give up the ghost until the ninth hour.

At that moment, a great calm fell over her, the knives vanished and with them all those unendurable emotions.

That was when she went mad.

Like a puppet, she followed Salome, Joseph's servant, as they carried the body to the rocky tomb in the garden. Joseph of Arimathea himself wrapped the thin shroud around the dead man. The soldiers watched and made sure the big stone was rolled across the entrance. Mary looked around the lovely garden, so full of peace. As they left, she took careful note of the way and whispered to Salome: 'We'll come here at dawn after the Sabbath to anoint him.'

'But the stone?'

Mary replied in her new cold voice, 'God must somehow help us.'

38

The water carrier's house was strangely unaltered. The women went quietly up to their room, and once there were at last able to weep, all except Mary Magdalene, who spread out her sleeping mat and fell asleep.

The silent weeping of the women around her deepened her sleep, now as black as pitch and with no images.

Then it was the morning of the Sabbath. They took their Passover meal, but could eat no more than crumbs of the good food. They went to bed early and then they were all able to sleep, Mary Magdalene as soundly as if unconscious, until she was awakened by the water carrier standing in the doorway.

'It's an earthquake,' he said. 'I have a protected room below the floor on the ground floor. Take your sleeping mats and go there.'

At that moment they felt the house shaking and the floor moving beneath their feet. Some screamed with fear, others began to collect up their things and run toward the stairs. Only Mary remained unmoved, in fact pleased. That's good, Jesus, shake up the world so that it at last understands what it has done.

But the water carrier hurried her, and last of all, she slowly went down the stairs to the cramped room under the house where the servants and the Greek woman had brought bread, cheese, olives, and water.

Mary Magdalene was the only one able to eat. Then she lay down on her mat and at once fell asleep. The mother of Jesus, Mary the wife of Clopa, and Salome, who had all endured at the foot of the cross with Mary Magdalene, did the same.

At dawn, she was awakened by Salome, who had bought spices and oil. They were generous with the fragrant spices as they prepared the olive oil that was to anoint his body.

Before daylight, they were on their way. The earthquake had subsided, but making their way along the alleys was difficult, for houses and walls had collapsed and people were desperately searching in the ruins for their lost relatives. No one noticed the two women climbing over collapsed shops, a spacious basket between them containing the linen cloth and precious oil and spices.

The town stank of shattered drains and rotting remains of food.

Then suddenly they were outside the wall, where the destruction was not so great, but there were plenty of fallen pillars and large stones.

Salome gasped. 'Do you remember,' she said. 'Yesterday

evening Mary Magdalene said that God would help us with the stone? Now you'll see.'

And it was just as she had said. When they reached the garden, they at once saw the great stone had rolled away from the entrance and down the slope. Best of all was that the earthquake had frightened away the Roman soldiers ordered to guard the tomb. The two women were alone in the garden when the first rays of the sun trickled through the treetops and the first birds began to sing. Mary Magdalene drew a deep breath and listened.

Despite everything, perhaps she was on her way back to herself, she thought.

They crept into the rocky tomb. A few thin rays of sunlight were making their way in through the opening, but it was still so dark, it took a moment or two for their eyes to get used to it.

It took them some time to grasp what they saw.

The rocky ledge on which they had laid the body was bare, nothing but the lovely shroud left behind.

'It's not possible,' whispered Salome. 'Not possible, not possible.'

Mary Magdalene was unable even to whisper, but then her great burden of grief at last caught up with her.

She wept, the tears welling up from inside her and pouring out with such force, she found it hard to breathe. Then her sobs took over, loud and inhuman.

More like screams than tears.

'Try to be quiet,' said Salome. 'No one must find us here.'

Mary's sobs slowly ceased, now only her tears still streaming down her face, as impossible to stop as the rain in the winter months.

'What do we do?'

'There's nothing to do here.'

'We must go back and tell them.'

'Yes.'

'Ssh, there's a man outside.'

Mary was not frightened. She would not hesitate, even if the entire Roman cohort was on guard outside the tomb.

A man was standing there. Although dazzled by the sunlight, almost painful to her eyes after the dark of the tomb, she could see him against the light. She thought it was one of Joseph's gardeners.

'Why weepest thou?' he said.

Mary tried to swallow her tears. 'If thou have borne him hence, tell me where you hast laid him, and I will take him away.'

'Mary,' said the man.

That very moment she knew the voice, that light voice she loved. The knowledge cut through her, transformed her, and she felt the clarity and strength restore her body, mind, and senses.

The wind rose, the morning wind whipping up the dust and leaves from the garden, which had been damaged by the earthquake. The picture of him blurred.

But the voice was clear and full of humour as he said: 'But go your way, tell his disciples and Peter that he goeth before thee into Galilee: there you will see him, as he said unto you.'

They ran, both of them, but had to stop at the town wall to get their breath back.

'But where shall we find them?' said Salome. 'They've not been here during all the difficult times.'

Mary Magdalene smiled. 'Jesus knew. We'll go to the water carrier's house.'

She was right. They were all there, in the big room at the top of the house, paralyzed with grief and impotence. Naturally, they did not want to believe her, but finally Peter rose and went off toward the empty tomb.

39

In her house in Antioch, Mary Magdalene sat putting down her memories in writing on parchment.

She had been doing it for two days and Leonidas was worried over her tiredness, her stomach pains and pallor. Late that afternoon, Peter and Paul came to see them to say farewell before their long journey to the congregations in Thessalonica.

It was a relief.

'I'll write a letter to you and tell you everything I can remember about the resurrection,' she said.

Paul looked pleased and Peter gave her a great bear hug and thanked her. They all said at once that they would soon be seeing each other again.

Leonidas went with them to the gate, and when he came back he saw the colour had come back to her face and she had straightened up. Then he told her he had just loaded a ship that was to sail to Corinth.

'You wanted to go there,' he said.

Mary smiled at him and her 'yes' was large and sunny.

She was told they were to sail as soon as the end of the week. So she had only a short time for the letter to Paul. Mary thought that did not matter, she would write briefly and factually to describe what she had seen and experienced.

'You know they say you saw an angel in the tomb,' said Leonidas.

'No, I didn't know that. I shall write that it's not true. I shall also spare him that my emotions were split in two at Golgotha. And my madness when I sought him out in Galilee.'

'That's good, nothing personal.'

'No, I promise.'

The letter was not short. She was thorough about every detail, and factual.

She added a postscript.

'You know that I met him yet once again, in a vision. What he said that day you have already heard many times over. 'Make no laws . . .'

On the Friday morning, the ship departed from Seleucia, the sails filled by the wind and Mary with a new happiness.

Part Four

40

They had a good east wind and the heavily-loaded ship almost danced across the seas, wind singing in the sails and waves slapping against the hull. But as they sailed below the mountains of Peloponnesus and set course north, it turned almost solemnly calm. For a moment.

Then the great sail crackled as the oarsmen put all their strength into the turn, others sheeted, and slowly the sail filled with the light breeze from starboard.

Leonidas gazed out across the water and said to Mary, 'The Aegean always makes me think of your eyes.'

'Oh, no, no eyes are that blue.'

She had rested a great deal during the voyage, sleeping long into the mornings.

But one day he had awakened her early.

'Come on now, sleepyhead, up you get and come and see the quays of Cenchree.'

She dressed quickly. Inside the mole in the long bay lay the harbour town with its warehouses, and there, in the swarm on the quay, Euphrosyne was waiting. They would soon be meeting, and not until the ship glided in to the lee below the mole did Mary realize how much she had been longing to see her stepmother.

Then they caught sight of her, standing there with a horse and carriage in all the noise and confusion on the quay, Setonius in the driving seat. Mary had to blink back her tears.

It was warm, but not hot, the sea wind cooling the air.

Euphrosyne came on board and they stood as they usually did, holding each other's hands, their eyes scrutinizing each other's faces.

'You've changed,' said Euphrosyne finally.

'I have much to tell you. But you are the same. You don't age.'

'No. When I thought I'd aged enough, I put a stop to it.'

Leonidas appeared at that moment, the only one with no respect for Euphrosyne's distance. He took her in his arms and gave her such a hug, it pained both her chest and her soul.

'My children,' she said. And the next moment: 'Don't let's be sentimental.'

'No,' said Leonidas. 'I haven't time. I've a great deal to do.'

He went off to the harbour office and in customary fashion bribed his way through customs. Within an hour began the unloading of the silk that was to go to Corinth, a third of the cargo, the rest destined for Ostia; then the ship was to sail as soon as the next morning.

'But you've time to have dinner with me?'

'Of course. And I won't be away for long. I'll be back to fetch Mary in a few weeks.'

When he saw a shadow flit across Mary's face, he added: 'If you don't want to stay any longer, of course.'

She shook her head in confusion.

Down on the quay, Mary embraced Setonius, now aged and looking like a wise old man. Quite right, Mary thought, for that's just what he is.

They drove through the new town, past side roads down which they could just glimpse the huge temple ruins of the old Corinth the Romans had burned down and plundered.

Then there it was, just as it should be, Euphrosyne's lovely house clinging to the hillside, where the high mountains softened toward the Bay of Corinth. They were welcomed with wine on the terrace and sat gazing out across the sea, listening to the waves breaking against the stone-laid quay.

After the meal, Leonidas had to leave. Euphrosyne was given another great bear hug, but he held Mary long and gently in his arms, his eyes not meeting hers, the heavy eyelids lowered.

'That man does not earn his money easily,' said Euphrosyne as they waved him off and were on their way back to the house. 'He seems worn out and weary.'

Anxiety and self-reproach washed over Mary like a wave. Had she even noticed Leonidas these last few months? They had talked a lot, but only about her and her problems.

Euphrosyne went on. 'He also has a lot of trouble with that son-in-law revelling around and misappropriating the firm's money. Do you know how the divorce is going?'

Mary shook her head. She had forgotten all about Nicomachus and had not listened particularly carefully when Livia and Leonidas had talked about the difficulties in getting a divorce from an absent husband. She had not even gone to see Mera and the child. How were they?

Mary sat in silence as Euphrosyne persisted. 'Leonidas is getting old. He must be well over sixty now.'

'I never think about it.' Mary was ashamed. 'Remember I once told you I lack empathy?' she said finally.

'You've changed. That isn't true any longer.'

Mary could not stop her tears. 'I learned so much from you, your caring for everyone and your sense of responsibility. And then, when I went to Capernaum, you never had a word of reproach.'

'Here's a handkerchief,' said Euphrosyne.

Mary blew her nose and pulled herself together. 'Not that I wish to defend myself, but it has been a trying time. If you could bear it, I'd like you to read the notes on my talks with Simon Peter and Paul.'

'Paul?' said Euphrosyne, and Mary could hear she was surprised.

She went up to her room to unpack, a lovely room, high

ceilinged and with a long balcony, as white as white, bright blue covers on the bed and a view over a bay as wide as a sea. She picked up her case of papyrus scrolls and took them down to where Euphrosyne was resting in the shade on the terrace.

'I'll read them,' she said. 'You go unpack and take a rest.'

Mary tried to relax, but her conscience was troubling her. She had indeed known that Leonidas had had difficulties, and sorrows. He had pulled himself together and had left that self-absorbed boy, his lover of several years standing. One evening he had mentioned it. In passing. And Mary had felt relief. The beautiful boy had demeaned Leonidas.

But not for a moment had she given a thought as to how hard taking that step must have been.

Nor had she thought about Leonidas being twenty years older than she.

Perhaps she still regarded him as a father who would provide her with consolation and security. She flushed with shame when she remembered what she had said to Paul about how important it was to free yourself from your parents.

To become an adult yourself.

Then she thought that if Leonidas really had been her father, she would have taken greater care of him.

She had no peace of mind, so could not rest. She got up and went out onto the balcony. Down in the garden, she could see Setonius and his labourers and decided to go and take a look at his work.

On previous visits, she had always thought the garden was very like the old one on the shores of the Gennesaret. Here, too, was the fine contrast between enclosed spaces and wide views.

'You're an artist, Setonius,' she said.

He brightened and was proud and eloquent as he showed her around. They discussed roses and Mary complained that hers suffered badly from the heat in Antioch.

'And the wind,' said Setonius. 'That's a windy site you have. How are the irises doing? And the gardenia you were given?'

'The irises only just survive. But the gardenia died long ago.'

He sighed. 'It's hard struggling against nature.'

Then he looked at her and after some hesitation said, 'Did you hear about Octavianus?'

'Yes, Euphrosyne wrote to tell me.'

'He died. He was ill for only a few days . . . and we probably didn't take it all that seriously. You know how he used to exaggerate.'

Mary smiled as she recalled Octavianus trying to make her eat with the most hideous threats. 'He had dramatic talents,' she said.

'Yes, an actor. Come, I'll show you his grave.'

Octavianus had been buried by the wall facing the sea, the grave covered with flowering herbs and lush green vegetables, a large pumpkin hanging over the headstone.

'I thought he'd like it here,' said Setonius.

Mary nodded, then her eyes fell on the cross against the wall, and Setonius noticed. 'Yes,' he said. 'Octavianus became Christian, burning with faith.'

As they left the grave to inspect the vegetable beds, Mary asked, 'But you stick to your old gods, do you?'

'Yes, they'll have to do for me. They're closer to nature. And they are still alive today and roam around on earth here. If one is humble and observant, maybe they'll stay for a while and listen.'

Mary nodded. She understood. Then she thought that if anyone had presence and love, then it was Setonius.

'Jesus would also have stopped to listen to you.'

'Me, a stubborn old heathen!'

Setonius laughed before going on. 'Here among the Christians of Corinth, someone like me is condemned to a fiery hell. Whatever that is.'

'That's lying talk,' said Mary.

As she went back to the house, she was thinking that her self-appointed task of giving other people interpretations of what Jesus had taught was meaningless, a single cry in the darkness, and when she reached the terrace and saw that Euphrosyne had read all her notes, that thought was confirmed.

'You've been ambitious, Mary. But over the ages mankind has had a great many great new thinkers. And only very few people have understood what they said. Most have been misunderstood and adapted to prevailing prejudices.'

Mary nodded. Euphrosyne smiled her crooked smile.

'Here in town, Paul is an important man and has a great deal to offer. We can partake of the flesh and blood of Christ every Sunday and find consolation for all wretchedness in solemn rituals and incomprehensible devotions. The price is reasonable, most people think, only submission and loss of individual thought. Do as the new church says and everything will go well for you.'

Mary said nothing for a long spell.

'So you mean this was all in vain,' she said finally, pointing at her scrolls.

'No, I think they're important, very important in fact. I suggest we have them copied and keep the copies in my vault in the cellar.'

'I thought you'd become a Christian,' said Mary.

'So I did. For quite a while. I was even a member of Paul's congregation. But the price was too high for me. I thought too much and asked too many questions . . . to put it briefly, I and other women here became thorns in the side of the apostle.'

'To express it in the Jewish way,' she added, laughing.

Then she looked surprised. 'Perhaps I am Christian at heart. I was thinking that as I was reading what you've written. It was his parables as you heard them that made an impression.'

Mary was so pleased, she almost cried.

'You really have become quite maudlin,' said Euphrosyne, but her voice was full of tenderness.

At dinner, Euphrosyne told her the story of a young man who fell in love with his equally young stepmother, a girl who had been brutally given away to a rich old orthodox Jew.

'She was raped in the customary marital way, night after night. She wasted away and lamented, and one day she said to her stepson that she· was going to walk into the sea. He tried to comfort her and as he did so, they were both overcome by love.

'The story was soon out around town, growing and growing and flourishing in every man's mouth. The old man's verdict was totally without mercy – she was to be stoned. The family had all been christened and strangely enough several members of the congregation spoke of mercy. The old man was disliked, so that probably added to it. Perhaps there was a streak of Jesus' gentleness in their minds, I don't know. Otherwise the congregation is constantly squabbling. Apostles quarrel just like rabbis.'

She sighed before going on with her story.

'After a while, the congregation split into two camps, hitting each other over the head with quotes from the scriptures. In the end they agreed – the question of the young couple was to be referred to Paul. After endless discussions on the wording, a message was sent off with the letter to Macedonia, where the apostles were.'

Euphrosyne sighed, took a gulp of wine and went on. 'The answer came swiftly back and was unambiguous. I'll read it to you.'

She left the dining room, headed for the library and came back with a copy of Paul's letter.

'Listen to this: "It is reported commonly that there is fornication among you . . . but ye are puffed up, and have not rather mourned . . . might be taken away from among you. I have judged already . . . in the name of our Lord Jesus Christ to deliver such a one to Satan for the destruction of the flesh . . ."'

Euphrosyne slapped the table before going on. 'That same

197

night, the two young people walked into the sea. And the next day, I left the congregation.'

In the light of the lamp, Mary noticed her stepmother was looking exhausted. 'We must sleep,' she said.

'Yes, it's been a long day.'

'Have you any more copies of Paul's letters? May I read them?'

'Of course. Read them before you go to sleep. Perhaps you'll take a different view of Paul from that of the good listener in Antioch.'

Before they parted for the night, Euphrosyne said, 'Have you considered that neither Peter nor Paul asked about what the relationship was between you and Jesus?'

'As you see, I avoided saying anything. Simon Peter knew. And Paul never even touched on the subject.'

'But why not?'

Mary laughed. 'But it's obvious, Euphrosyne. Their God was not allowed to need a woman.'

41

Mary spent all night reading the letters. She was not so upset as Euphrosyne had been, either by the many rules for the righteous or the severe judgments on the unrighteous. They were all familiar from her childhood synagogues.

Like the contempt for women.

Women, the gateway to the Devil.

Leonidas used to say that it was fear of love between men and women that was reflected in the messages and Mary considered that a friendly interpretation. She went back to the letters.

Despite everything, it was better to marry than to burn, she read. Women who appeared with their heads uncovered might just as well shave off their hair. Man, on the other hand, needed no headgear, as he was an image of God.

Shame on a woman who speaks in assembly. If she wants to know something, she must ask her husband once they are home.

With some bitterness, Mary remembered Magdala, where her brothers could go to school and she was not even allowed to ask what they had learned.

Then she smiled slightly, imagining Euphrosyne and all those questions she must have put to Paul.

A moment later she found a very strange passage. He wrote that he had bad times, been beaten, suffered shipwreck, starved, and thirsted. In exchange, he had received great revelations, but in order not to boast about such things he had a thorn in his flesh, an angel of Satan who prevented arrogance.

She closed her eyes and pictured the tormented figure, bowed and stumbling as he made his way down the hill by her house. What kind of illness did he suffer from?

But what interested her most was the theology he had constructed around Jesus. By one man sin entered the world, and death by sin, and so death passed upon all men, for all have sinned. For until the law sin was in the world: but sin is not imputed when there is no law. For as by one man's disobedience many were made sinners, so by the obedience of one shall many be made righteous. For the wages of sin is death, but the gift of God is eternal life through Jesus Christ our Lord.

How magnificent, she thought without irony. But she could not make Paul's vision fit in with the young man she had loved.

In the end she read about love: Charity suffereth long and is kind . . . charity vaunteth not itself, is not puffed up . . . beareth all things . . . endureth all things.

And she learned the conclusion by heart: For now we see through a glass darkly . . . but then face to face . . . now I know in part . . . but then shall I know even as also I am known . . .

And now abideth faith, hope, and charity, these three, but the greatest of these is charity.

She prayed for Leonidas before she fell asleep.

Mary and Euphrosyne talked all the next morning.

They had a lot to catch up on.

Mary told Euphrosyne about Terentius and his wife, Cipa, who had had her tongue cut out as a child. 'She's a secretive girl, and I found it difficult not being able to talk to her. But one day when she was cleaning my workroom, I caught her taking a secret look at my notes. Cipa was afraid, but I was pleased and said: "Can you read?"'

Nod. '"But Cipa, then we can talk to each other. You write and I'll answer in speech."'

'A strange friendship grew between us. Every midday, Cipa came with a number of written questions and I took them one at a time and answered them fully. They could be about practical matters or about God and what he might have intended with her tongue. But I also asked questions and learned a lot more about the Gnostic faith.

'It was good for me,' Mary said to Euphrosyne. 'I was made to think in a new way. She is so innocent.'

'I see.'

'She has a sense of humour, too. Isn't that strange? There's always laughter lying in wait behind her closed mouth. She seems to have lived in a secret corner of life, observing and enjoying the comedy we all act out.'

Euphrosyne laughed and said she did not think that at all strange.

She told Mary about her new cook, the exact opposite of Octavianus, silent and serious. His dishes were not flavoured with words about how divinely good they were; on the contrary. 'I'm sorry, but it became a bit salt.' Which was not true. He cooked excellent food, as Mary must already have noticed.

'The only time he lets words fly is when he quarrels with his wife,' said Euphrosyne. 'That happens regularly once a week and the sharp words and clatter of pans and dishes echo all over the house. He's happier then and more voluble,' Euphrosyne said and she laughed as she added: 'Quite a lot of earthenware gets smashed, as you can imagine.'

At breakfast, Mary was told her stepmother had prepared a surprise. As they sat chatting on the terrace, they heard a carriage on its way up toward the house.

'Mary, go up to your room and brush your hair. Put on your blue tunic and come down in a minute. We've got company.'

Mary obedyed.

As she ran down the stairs, she heard the voices of two women deep in confidential conversation, one Euphrosyne's, and the other . . . ? She recognized it, gruff, joyous. But who, from where did she remember it? Her heart suddenly began to thump.

She stopped and stood still for a moment, then slipped over to the wide door out on to the terrace. In the most comfortable chair in the house sat an old lady, slightly hunched, but grandly dressed and dignified.

'Susanna!' cried Mary, so loudly the birds rose from the trees, and the next moment she was on her knees by the old lady with her face buried in her lap.

'Susanna,' she cried again and again. 'Can it be true, is it really you?'

The old lady cautiously ran her hand over the fair hair. 'My child,' she said. 'My little child.'

Mary wept and wept, so much, Euphrosyne had to tell her to calm down. It was no use, Mary just went on crying: 'Susanna, Susanna.'

Euphrosyne's voice sharpened. 'Mary, Susanna is old. All this excitement does her no good.'

That helped. Mary fell silent, but stayed where she was, holding the old lady's hands. 'Are you still as clever with your needle?' she asked.

'No, some things are lost over the years.'

Euphrosyne had wine brought in, despite the early hour, and she poured it out. She said they were all to take a drink and calm down. Susanna drank and the colour came back to her face. Mary sipped a little of hers and yet seemed intoxicated.

'Where did you go?' said Susanna, with no hint of reproach, and Mary knew the question had to be asked and answered.

'I went mad,' she said simply.

When she saw the other woman's surprise, she felt she had chosen the wrong word. 'My mind just went,' she said.

Her words made the two women sit up and Mary thought perhaps she had never told Euphrosyne.

She began with Golgotha and how she had been split in two as they had waited below the cross, one part empty, incapable of either thinking or feeling, and the other, the usual, containing a life-threatening agony.

'I didn't become whole again until the third day, when I met Jesus by the tomb. You remember how Salome and I came running back with the news to the water carrier's house, and there you all were, even the men who had dared come down from the mountains. A day or so later I had a second vision, when he said: "Make no laws . . ." And then the dispute with Peter and the break when he threw me out, us . . .

'Then the split in my mind came back, and somehow it saved me. I simply escaped into the emptiness. I had but one thought. I would meet Jesus in Galilee. It was stupid, but the only thing in that emptiness. I remember nothing about how I left town, or about the long walk to Galilee.

'You must see, my memory had gone. All of you, and all I'd been part of, Euphrosyne and Leonidas – it had all just disappeared.'

She told them how she had begged her way there, slept under the open sky, though occasionally in a sheep hut, the ashes in her hair, the sores, dirt, and neglect.

'Leonidas found me much much later. I was sleeping on the shore of the Gennesaret. He washed me, found a doctor, and took me with him to the sea. There he kept on talking to me to get my head going again. I slowly recovered, and began to get used to the idea of being the wife of a merchant.

'Then I was in my house in Antioch for years, reading books, training my mind, and filling my head with knowledge. But it took a long time before I found the courage to remember, and even then I had to let it happen slowly and carefully. Oh, I was so frightened, Susanna.'

'Of madness?' said Euphrosyne.

'Yes. It's terrible to lose your mind.'

They stayed there for a long time, looking out over the garden and the sea.

Susanna's voice was gruff when she broke the silence. 'We searched for you for days in Jerusalem, the other women and I. We went up and down all the alleys and asked wherever we dared. In the end we sat in a grove on the Mount of Olives and told ourselves you were dead, that you had followed the man you loved.

'Eventually we all returned, each to her own. But we wrote to each other and once a year we met in someone's home and reminded each other what Jesus had said and done during those years. And Lydia wrote down our memories.'

'Is Lydia still alive?'

'Yes, she and Salome live with me in Ephesus. Most of them are still alive, Mary.'

Mary Magdalene closed her eyes, making an effort to grasp that they all existed, that they had done as she had, shaped their own memories far away from the apostles and their teachings.

Susanna went on: 'One day we went to the synagogue in Ephesus to listen to the famous Paul. He was a disappointment, an insignificant man, we thought. Afterward there was a lot of talk about him, and a Jew said that there was a rumour that Paul had carried on conversations in Antioch with Mary Magdalene.

'At first I thought that was nonsense, but I knew the man who had talked of you and couldn't let the matter drop. So I went to him and asked. He was certain. You were alive and married to a silk merchant in Antioch.

'Then I suddenly remembered the Greek Leonidas and recalled that he came from Syria. When I went home to the others, I was so excited the words came tumbling out of me.

'Then Lydia remembered that you had talked about your stepmother and that her name was Euphrosyne and she lived in Corinth. We wrote a letter to her. And had an answer that said we were welcome to stay with her in September when her daughter, Mary of Magdala, was to visit her.'

Susanna laughed. 'It surprises me we didn't have a stroke, the joy of that letter arriving,' she said.

Euphrosyne said perhaps they had had enough for the moment. They had a light dinner and then Mary went with Susanna to her room to help her to bed.

'Why didn't the others come with you?' she whispered.

'We have a shop and someone has to see to it. I was the one they could most easily do without.'

The days of calm went by quickly. Susanna slept a lot and Mary wrote a long letter to Salome and Lydia. It was not easy. She was driven by a need to account for everything, all those many long years. In the end she also wrote of the future, at least the near future. She would persuade Leonidas to call in at Ephesus on the way home, she wrote. Then they would make a plan together on how their cooperation could continue.

When the scribe was to copy Mary's notes, Mary asked for an extra copy that Susanna could take back with her to the other two.

Mary found it hard to sleep at night. Everything that had happened and her anxiety over Leonidas plagued her, nor was it any better when he returned. He was pale and tired and kept clasping his chest. 'I've peculiar pains around my heart,' he said.

The next day Euphrosyne summoned her doctor, a conscientious man, a Greek. He didn't like the sound of Leonidas' heart, but considered a long rest would help. What was most important was that he got home and was looked after by his own doctor.

Leonidas fell asleep while the doctor was still there.

Mary realized that no detour to Ephesus would come about. She bade Susanna a lengthy farewell and gave her the letter and a well-filled purse. 'A gift from me to the three of you,' she said. 'You'll hear from me as soon as possible.'

Susanna was to stay on in the house in Corinth for a few more weeks.

'Don't worry,' said Euphrosyne. 'I'll go with her to Ephesus to make sure she gets there safely.'

'We'll write, we'll write.'

42

On their voyage home, Leonidas seemed better, sleeping at night with Mary's hand in his, his colour improved, and she coaxed him into eating. They could talk to each other again. She said it was due to the sea air. He said it was due to her.

But then one morning, just as they had their first glimpse of the Orontes, Leonidas became very out of breath and his heart started racing. Mary was at a loss, for there was nothing she could do.

'Try taking deep breaths.'

But he could not, and the next moment he lost consciousness. Then just as suddenly as they had come, the pains in his chest went away and he fell asleep.

But God in heaven, how pale he was.

Livia, Mera, and her little boy were all waiting at the harbour in Seleucia, Livia full of energy and curiosity over the results of the voyage. Mary persuaded Leonidas to stay in his bunk and went ashore on her own.

'No one is to make demands on you now,' she had said, expecting some protest, but he smiled gratefully, and that only increased her anxiety.

She briefly explained to Livia that Leonidas was ill, and that they must summon his doctor immediately and meet him back at the house.

'Ill?'

'His heart.'

'Like Father,' whispered Livia.

Back at home, the days and nights were long in the cool bedroom.

The doctor said much the same as his colleague had in Corinth, only slightly more directly. 'His heart is worn out.'

They were given medicine, but it was little use.

Leonidas liked soups. Cipa boiled meat and rendered down strong stock into bouillon and Mary flavoured it and added vegetables. They tried fish, but the smell nauseated Leonidas. Mary wondered whether he had never liked fish but had pretended for her sake.

'I'll speak to the sisters at the temple of Isis,' said Mera.

Mary nodded.

A day or two later, a palanquin arrived outside the gate and Mary smiled at the aged priestess with relief and hope. The old woman wanted to be alone with Leonidas and she sat in his room, running her hands over his body while Mary waited outside with thumping heart.

'He'll go soon,' she said, when she came out. 'With joy and without hesitating. There's nothing I can do. He has decided, but I can alleviate his pain so that the days will be more bearable.'

She showed Mary a large flask full of a dark liquid.

'What is it?'

'Digitalis, from the foxglove' said the old priestess. 'In moderate doses. Give him three spoonfuls a day. It is not a cure, but it relieves.'

Mary thanked her and the old lady made her farewells. 'What must happen, will happen,' she said. 'When it's over, you are welcome to come and see me.'

Mary had to go via the kitchen to wash the tears from her face before going back to Leonidas, who smiled at her and said it was a remarkable witch she had found.

'Yes, and she brought a remarkable witch's brew with her. Let's try it.'

His heavy eyelids blinked with amusement, but he obediently opened his mouth when she offered him the first spoonful of digitalis. A moment later he was asleep and she sat quietly by his side. She could see he was breathing more easily and some colour had slowly come back into his face.

When he woke, he sat up for the first time for several days. 'I'm hungry. Soup. And where's that miracle medicine?'

Mary thought about the old priestess' words: 'doesn't cure, just relieves,' but she said nothing. Then she thought about the stately foxgloves in her garden, long since dead. She had never known they had such strength.

She had her bed taken into Leonidas' room and slept spasmodically, listening to his breathing, thinking a lot, remembering, in all her despair able to feel gratitude to him.

I never said how much I loved him.

He was always worse when daylight came.

'Medicine, Mary,' he hissed.

That helped him through the mornings. Then his strength failed again and it would take another spoonful for him to be able to get a little dinner down.

They were occasionally able to talk in the afternoons and she spoke of their love and everything he had meant to her.

'One of the strangest love stories in the world,' he said, winking at her with amusement.

Livia came, tiptoed to her brother and sat quietly for a while. Rabbi Amasya came, knelt at his bedside, and prayed. Leonidas slept most of the time. At night, Mary sometimes wept in her sleep and woke him.

'It hurts me that you're sad,' he said, with difficulty. 'You're well provided for in my will,' he added.

'Leonidas,' she almost snapped at him, and that was the only time she raised her voice during his long illness. He smiled and looked ashamed.

'Try to get Euphrosyne to come,' he whispered.

Mary shook her head.

But when Livia came for her afternoon visit, he emerged from his sleep. 'See to it that Euphrosyne comes,' he whispered. 'I don't want Mary to be alone when I leave her.'

'I promise,' said Livia.

Days and nights merged into each other, the first blessed rains came, but Mary did not notice. The only moments she had to herself were when Terentius cared for Leonidas, helped him empty his bowels, washed his body, and changed the sheets. Then Mary went to the bathroom and sometimes had time to take a bath. But she mostly stayed sitting beside him.

She could no longer weep.

'Mary,' Leonidas said one night. 'I want you to promise me one thing.'

'Yes.'

'I want you to swear to it.'

'Yes.'

'You are not to go into that emptiness.'

'I promise. I swear I won't.'

Another night, he said, 'I often dream about Jesus, that he's here in the light.'

'He is,' whispered Mary.

Then she lay awake, thinking that she could not feel that presence.

Nor did she see any light. The darkness was dense outside and Leonidas wanted no lamp in the room. She had a little bowl of oil on her bedside table and the flame glinted like old silver.

But at dawn that day, she was awakened by the light Leonidas had talked about, the whole room dazzlingly white. She leaned over him and at once knew he had gone.

She had no memory of the following few days, only one thing on her mind, reminding her every evening of her promise to Leonidas: 'I must not give way to that emptiness.'

43

As neither Leonidas nor Mary had ever had much to say about Mary's stepmother, Livia had formed a picture of her own – a simple woman, a Greek peasant girl who for some unfathomable reason had married a Jew and soon been widowed in barbaric Palestine.

A marriage of that kind indicated a person with no sense.

Then she had settled in a house in Tiberias, a vulgar settler town in Galilee. That was where she had undertaken to look after the child. She was undoubtedly a clever housekeeper and had somehow probably made the dead Jew's money go around.

Leonidas had paid for Mary's education, the learned Greek teachers. Her brother had revealed that one evening when he had drunk too much and Livia had said something encouraging about how well educated Mary was.

I suppose it's always so, Livia thought, that mothers shape their daughters. And what Mary had learned in the house in Tiberias was obvious: cooking, looking after a garden, being careful with money, and being humble and grateful.

Consequently, Livia detested Euphrosyne long before they ever met. She also had sufficient troubles of her own without having an unknown relative around her neck. The poor state of the firm's finances, the absent Nicomachus, Leonidas' will, then the funeral and all the work that had entailed.

But Livia had promised her brother she would bring the stepmother there.

Mary was no help. She went around like a ghost, did not reply when spoken to, and had neither opinions nor desires.

One morning, it occurred to Livia that the small-minded Euphrosyne in Corinth had accepted her invitation because she wanted to watch over Mary's and her own interests at the distribution of the estate.

Of course. That was it.

But as they stood there down at the harbour watching the ship arriving, Livia was ashamed when she saw the joy lighting up Mary's face as she waved to the passengers, crying out: 'Oh, Mother, Mother, Mother . . .'

Then Livia spotted the tall woman at the railing, and she clutched at Mera's arm – hold on to me. But she was still feeling shaken as the elegant woman walked down the gangway and took Mary into her arms.

'We'll survive this time, too,' Euphrosyne said to her stepdaughter.

Mary straightened up, and once again there was hope in her eyes.

But Livia was wondering what the stepmother had meant with those words.

Euphrosyne greeted her in a friendly but slightly polite way.

She spoke classic Greek, too, with no trace of dialect. She's a woman of the world, Livia thought. Why didn't anyone tell me?

Later, Euphrosyne thanked the Roman captain for their good journey. Her luggage was to be taken to Mary's house, but Livia wanted to welcome them with dinner at hers. She had made a great effort over the numerous dishes and fine wines. An amused smile crossed Euphrosyne's face, and Livia loathed her.

After the guests had left, Livia went to bed. She was deathly tired after everything that had happened. But she had managed the funeral, which had taken place according to Greek rituals. The mourning feast afterward, too, and all the consoling words to the employees, who were fearful for the future. The money?

Everything depended on the will, which was to be read the next day.

Mary had been central to Leonidas and the risk that paying out her inheritance would ruin the firm was great.

She missed her brother, by all the gods how she missed him, his laughter and his energy.

'I liked her,' said Euphrosyne on their way to Mary's house. 'But what is she frightened of?'

'The will – it means the whole of the inheritance goes to me. I have to tell you the family firm is her life's work.'

At Mary's, the guest house that had once been equipped for Mera and her child had been put in order. Euphrosyne was to be made comfortable, almost as she was used to. She greeted Cipa with curiosity and Terentius with respect. Everything was to her satisfaction, she said, thanking them for their care. Terentius thought, as Livia had, a lady, a real lady.

They did not say much as they went through the garden and Mary was ashamed of the ravages caused by the heat. When they got back to the house, Mary asked Terentius for mulled wine.

'It helps you sleep,' she said.

'Do you sleep badly?'

'No, I sleep whenever I get a chance.'

'But you're eating badly, I can see that. And I think with horror about the time when . . . Leonidas died the previous time. We have no Octavianus now.'

'I'll try to do better.'

'Good.'

Mary ate some of the browned chicken and freshly baked bread, so much, her body felt heavy.

They said goodnight.

A long day was over, and Mary slept like a child. Like the child I am, she thought. Father is dead but Mother will look after me.

As usual, Euphrosyne was up at the crack of dawn and with pen and paper, she sat down at the kitchen table and said to Cipa: 'I'm worried about Mistress Mary's poor appetite. We must get her to eat.'

Cipa took her time, then picked up the pen and wrote briefly, 'You can trust me.'

Euphrosyne was very pleased.

When Mary appeared, she was almost swollen with sleep. 'I can't tell you how well I slept.'

'We've quite a few things to talk about. But eat your breakfast first.'

Mary stayed at the kitchen table and Cipa served a very strange meal, fat cheese and salt olives, a large pear, bread, and cold beer.

'I know just who has been talking to you,' Mary said to Cipa, and she ate like a hungry child.

A little while later, Euphrosyne told her about her visit to Ephesus, about Salome, Lydia, and Susanna, who lived a thrifty life in two small rooms above their little shop.

'They had something. Peace and a naturalness,' she said, after some seeking for the words. Then she went on. 'What are you going to do with your inheritance?'

'Leave it in the firm.'

They smiled at each other. Cipa noticed and was pleased.

Then the man with the will and endless piles of documents arrived. He had been in the service of the family for many years and was thorough and cold, as befits a lawyer.

He began by accounting for the firm's assets, the ships, the silk-weaving mill, outstanding claims, the houses.

The debts were also considerable, he said. One difficulty concerned the absent son-in-law, who might appear at any moment and bankrupt the whole firm by agreeing to the divorce. He did not look at Mera as he said it, but all of them around the table felt the chill in his voice.

There was a solemn silence as he broke the seal around the will.

Naturally it was just as Livia had feared, Leonidas' entire fortune was to go to Mary.

Mary spoke, turning calmly and considerately to Livia. 'I have decided to let my money remain in the firm. We will be part owners, you and I. You will have to take on all the responsibility and do all the work, unjust, I know, but you know I have no head for business. And I am going to move back home to my mother's as soon as I have sold the house.'

Once Livia had regained her powers of speech, she said, 'What would Leonidas have said?'

'He would have burst out laughing,' said Euphrosyne.

Livia looked surprised, so Euphrosyne went on. 'I'm convinced that clever boy has arranged things just as he had thought would happen. He has assured Mary's upkeep without making difficulties for the firm.'

Even Livia dared smile, but then her features sharpened. 'I request that Mary appoint a good man to represent her interests in the firm,' she said.

'Where in God's name would I find anyone like that?'

'Perhaps I can help,' said the lawyer.

'No,' said Livia and Euphrosyne, almost in unison.

The lawyer was in a hurry to get back to his office, saying

there were many more documents to be drawn up. Euphrosyne thought perhaps he was afraid Mary might change her mind.

That afternoon, the three women were at last able to talk about Leonidas.

'You knew my brother?' Livia said to Euphrosyne.

'Yes, very well. And I liked him. We came to be very close when we shared the responsibility for the child.'

'There's so much we don't know about him.'

'Yes, he was a quiet man.'

Euphrosyne sat deep in thought, then told them what it had been like when he had died the first time.

'Mary was only a child, but she almost died of grief, by starving herself. It was awful. I thought I'd go mad with worry.'

'We had a message from the Roman army, too, informing us of his death,' said Livia. 'Then only about a month later, a dirty Bedouin appeared with the demand for the ransom. My husband flatly refused and he was head of the firm. They were dreadful years.'

They nodded. They understood.

'The women in our family have a tendency to marry the wrong men,' Livia said finally. 'Mother did, I did, and so did Mera, poor thing.'

'I can't say I don't recognize the situation,' said Euphrosyne.

44

Mary was walking slowly on the white marble along the colonnaded street in Ephesus. The houses were all beautiful, but the huge temple almost took her breath away. Full of admiration, she stood gazing at the goddess with her many breasts, surrounded by all the animals of field and forest, bulls, antelopes, flying sphinxes with female breasts, and then those gigantic bees, the symbol of Artemis.

Great, how great was Diana of the Ephesians.

The Greek artists, too, she thought, remembering Setonius' tale of the statues of divinities in their places on the island of his childhood.

There was a lesser goddess there, too, and Mary was surprised to find her face resembled that of Isis in the temple in Antioch. The great mother, now losing her power over the world, she thought, remembering the words of the old priestess.

A little later, she made her way to the outskirts of the town. It took some time, for the town was large, almost as large as Antioch. But so different, so much lighter, easier.

She was alone. Euphrosyne had objected and had said Terentius should go with her as her shadow and protector. But Mary did not want to arrive at her friends of all those years with a handsome slave in tow. She was wearing worn grey garments she had found at the bottom of the clothes chest when packing, and she had washed them and had Cipa mend the rips and holes. They were the same clothes she had worn during her wanderings with Jesus, and as she dressed before going ashore, to her great surprise, the patched but indestructible garments gave her new strength.

The ship with Euphrosyne and the servants on board had continued on to Corinth.

Mary had to ask her way to the poor street where Susanna, Lydia, and Salome lived. It was far away from the handsome centre of town, where Greeks from half the world strolled, made offerings to their gods, and enjoyed their beauty.

The streets here narrowed to alleys and just as Mary was thinking she was lost in the jumble of little shops and street stalls, she spotted their shop, a piece of blue silk in it glowing from far away. Mary recognized it. Euphrosyne had given that to Susanna, she thought.

She opened the door. Fortunately there were no customers, and behind the counter was Lydia, straight-backed, tall, and handsome. The two women looked at each other in silence, filled with solemnity and joy.

'May I sit down?' whispered Mary.

That was enough to rouse Lydia from her paralysis. She pulled up a chair and fetched a glass of water. 'Have you walked far?'

'Only from the harbour. But it's a big town.'

'Drink!'

'Thank you.'

Then Lydia banged on the ceiling with a long stick. Mary heard a door open and Lydia called out: 'Hurry, hurry. She's come.'

Salome came running down the stairs. Mary's eyes filled with tears, so that she could scarcely see, and Salome was in the same state.

Neither said a word.

How strange that we're almost shy of each other, Mary thought.

'I must go and see Susanna,' she said.

'Come.'

Susanna was sitting in the kitchen upstairs, her arms held out. Just as she had done in Corinth, Mary fell to her knees and buried her face in Susanna's robe. Susanna smiled with delight and chattered away about how pleased, how very pleased they were. And what a long time they had waited.

And hoped.

Light as a breeze, she smoothed the rough edges of their confusion and soon the four of them were all talking at once.

They went on until Susanna interrupted and cried out: 'Food. We'll have a feast.'

Lydia went down and closed the shop. Mary went with her to fetch her bag of night things and change of clothes.

Salome made the meal, smoked lamb with a sauce, the flavours all kindling memories in Mary – it was just as it had been around their campfires in the evenings, all those years ago.

They did not say much that first evening, simply exchanging small talk after they had laid down on their mats. Oh, how well Mary recognized that gentle female chatter, though it took her some time to find the right position on the uncomfortable sleeping mat. It was a long time since Leonidas' wife had slept on the floor.

The next morning, the talk became a flood, they had so much to tell each other. At first, it was personal, about children and grandchildren and the rejoicing when they had gone back to their homes and could relate what had happened.

Mary sat in silence, knowing she had to tell them. 'My husband died a month ago.'

They put their arms around her and wept for her, their grief far far away from Euphrosyne's matter-of-factness and Livia's self-control.

They had many memories of Leonidas, and they talked about the day he had come to Capernaum, how handsome he was and how friendly and open.

'He had an amazing laugh,' said Lydia. 'I remember that it took everyone with him, both Simon, who was so mindful of his dignity, and those zealots who became our misfortune.'

They fell silent.

'I've never understood what happened,' said Mary.

'Let's leave it until morning,' said Salome. 'It's the Sabbath and we can spend the whole day on . . . our memories. We've read the copies of what you wrote, Mary. But we've also got notes Lydia has taken over the years. You can read them while we do what we have to do.'

'Thank you.'

While the women cleaned the house and shop and went out into town to shop for the Sabbath, Mary sat at the kitchen table and read. Their memories were different from hers in many details, but what was so wonderful was how similarly they had regarded the words and deeds of Jesus.

I was not as alone as I thought.

All the next day, they wove together their accounts, Mary's images with Lydia's notes. It strengthened them. They received confirmation, but Lydia told them how capricious memory was, all the same.

'For me, a memory can appear in a dream. It can be about a light over the lake, or the scent of a flower. Only sometimes is it a clear picture and someone saying something. Everything reminds me. When I wake, I try to make the picture clearer. I remember. But I become uncertain, where do I fill in and what do I add, what am I interpreting?'

Mary nodded. She recognized that.

But old Susanna laughed. 'You've too vivid an imagination,' she said. 'I remember what I remember and can go back whenever I want to, up the steps to the house in Capernaum, see the worn latch, stand there a moment listening to that young voice from the lake, as he sat there in the boat speaking to the people.'

'But that's amazing,' said Mary. 'Can you do that whenever you want to?'

'No. Usually it's when the memory has something to do with pain. I can see every detail of Golgotha, every event over those nine hours.'

'But that must mean there are things you find hard to remember,' said Salome. 'All the happinesses . . . ?'

Susanna nodded.

'It's strange,' said Mary. 'You were the one who was the happiest.'

This time, the silence lasted a long time. Salome went to fetch apricot juice and beakers, and as she served it, Mary looked thoughtfully at her.

'But what about you, Salome?' she said. 'How do you remember? You were the one who always had the best head.'

'No, that was you.'

'Wrong, you had intelligence. I had common sense.'

They laughed.

'The first years after the crucifixion,' said Salome, 'I considered I had perfectly clear memories of everything Jesus said and did. But then all that great myth making started in the Christian congregations – the resurrection, the angels at the tomb, the mother who was a virgin. Now they've found a star over Bethlehem . . .' She hesitated, then went on. 'They talk and talk, his apostles, and who am I to dare maintain they are wrong and I am right? I have become so uncertain . . .'

They all nodded. They all felt inadequate.

But Lydia rose to her full height as she said: 'I believe in sagas, stories about gods and monsters and miracles, horrible sea creatures and angels. But when they start saying they are real, that all of it has happened in our world, then I lose faith.'

The others looked surprised, but Mary understood.

'None of us has any answer to just who he was and what his task was,' said Susanna.

'I think Mary is right,' said Salome, her voice gentle, but her eyes angry, 'when she says "He was too great for us". But there are plenty of people who have answers for everything – Peter, Barnabas, and Paul, just to name a few.'

Susanna clamped her mouth shut and mumbled, 'What did you say?'

'That no one ever listens to women.'

They said nothing, for they knew that was true.

'Someone will in the end,' said Lydia. 'And perhaps that's enough.'

Mary told them about the Christian association that had put itself outside the teachings of the apostles.

'I was at a Gnostic service . . .'

She described the drawing of lots before the service and drew a lively picture of the woman preacher and what she had said.

'I was veiled and all in black,' she said. 'Over all those years in Antioch, I was always afraid of being recognized. You can imagine how upset I was when the woman up there started quoting from my dispute with Peter at the water carrier's house in Jerusalem – word for word,' Mary went on, the surprise still in her voice. 'That was when I realized that words have a life of their own. And power.'

They had been listening intently, as well as with some astonishment.

They sat there, thinking about it.

At last Salome spoke. 'Perhaps it's important that we also submit our testimonies?'

'Yes,' said Mary. Then she explained her plan.

She had talked to her stepmother on their voyage from Antioch, she told them, and Euphrosyne was keen to help them. They were to build a house between the two green hills on the big site by the Bay of Corinth. Library, a bedroom each, and a large kitchen. It's beautiful,' she said.

'Money?'

'We are his disciples and will do as he taught us. We'll put our assets into a common purse and share everything.'

'But we have so little.'

'I happen to have a lot. And there must be some meaning in my inheritance from Leonidas.'

Mary could almost hear their thoughts in the long silence that followed.

Lydia was thinking it would be difficult to leave Ephesus, where she had felt at home for almost twenty years.

Susanna was thinking she was too old.

Salome was more practical and it was she who broke the silence. 'But what would we do all day?' she said. 'We can't just talk and write.'

Mary smiled. 'I thought we might be able to grow vegetables and earn money from that. And then gradually we could take in pupils, women interested in what we have to teach.'

Comments fell like heavy raindrops.

'We must think it over.'

'Yes.'

'When are you leaving?'

'The ship is picking me up in a week.'

'What kind of town is Corinth?'

'Smaller than here.'

'Many Romans?'

'Yes, and many Jews.'

'What would people think of us?'

'Did you ever think that when you were following Jesus?'

'Do you think Jesus supports your idea?'

'Yes.'

'We'll let you know.'

'It's hard to change your life.'

'It's hard to live here, too. We're getting older.'

They got no further that evening. They laid the table for the Sabbath meal, lit their candles, and said the old prayers. But all their thoughts were a long way away.

Mary had to leave Ephesus without an answer. She had no desire to press the hesitant and reckoned she probably did not have to. Sometimes she was quite sure. The decision had already been made.

In the kingdom of heaven, she thought. Just what went on living so powerfully within these women?'

When Mary went on board ship on the agreed day, they were all there and they held her hand as if they dared not let it go.

'If we don't . . .' said Susanna, her voice trembling. 'Will you still come and see us sometimes?'

'Yes, I will, I promise.'

'So you won't be too disappointed.'

'Yes, but that'll pass, like everything else.'

'It's strange we've become so irresolute,' said Lydia. 'When you think we once gave up everything and just followed the Master.'

Mary nodded. She had often thought about that, how incredibly strong these women were who had followed Jesus, not just leaving their families, but breaking with their whole tradition, the entire Jewish community. So much spitting, so much ridicule they had had to endure.

'But it was as if we had no choice,' said Salome.

Mary thought carefully and then replied. 'I don't think we have now, either. We have a task.'

They smiled hesitantly at her.

Then the captain called out that the ship was ready for departure. The women had to go ashore and they parted with clumsy words.

'We'll meet again.'

And Mary knew that it would come to pass.

26/1/01